HELLSTITCHER

SILVER SKYE

Copyright © 2024 Silver Skye

All rights reserved.

ISBN: 9798337880297

HELLSTITCHER

All Rights Reserved

Copyright © 2024 Silver Skye

This book may not be reproduced, transmitted, or stored in whole or in part by any means, including graphic, electronic, or mechanical without the express written consent of the author except in the case of brief quotations embodied in critical articles and reviews.

Author: Silver Skye

Editor: Jessica Meigs at Edits By Jessica

Cover Design: Nabin Karna (Fiverr)

Wicked Harvest Books
Grand Blanc, Michigan

smelkerkyle@gmail.com
jsmelker@hotmail.com

Wicked Harvest Books Production
Jerrod S. Smelker, LLC

Silver Skye (Kylan Skye Smelker) was made in a doll factory, among the thousands of other exact copies. When a diabolical enchantress took over the factory, she cursed every doll in the factory to become her ever-lasting slaves. Out of the thousands of dolls sentenced to torment, only Silver could withstand the full-fledged power of the mighty enchantress. In an act of defiance, Silver threw down his tools, and stabbed the enchantress in the heart whilst she slept. Since then, he's had to teach others the value of freedom, and now reaches to the hearts of his audience with tales of woe. As a budding author, he seeks to reignite the desire to read, as reading is the ultimate form of imagination, freedom, and peace. Though his days are numbered by the curse of the enchantress, he only lives for the ones closest to him.

Alternate Bio -

Silver Skye (Kylan Skye Smelker) is a new budding author coming out of Ionia, Michigan. He is son to Jerrod Smelker, the author of many stories, including the likes of "Nina" and "Wicked Harvest: Michigan Monsters & Macabre". He grew up in both Ionia, Michigan; and Perrinton, Michigan, each having their own qualities over the other. Only being 19 as of the publishing date, he doesn't have much experience with the whole writing ordeal but is looking to keep his stories coming.

Out of all places, he loves the busy roads and towering buildings of cities the most. He's primarily a city man, always wanting the places he goes to be close, though he can enjoy visiting the country from time to time.

Silver enjoys time with friends and family, like most, but primarily enjoys collecting particular toys as a hobby. He loves painting, collecting, photographing, and building with them. He's deeply connected with the music he listens to, mainly comprising of rock n' roll and heavy metal. He is a certified gamer as well, showing proficiency in games such as Halo, Terraria, Minecraft, Spelunky 2, and most of all, Pokémon.

DEDICATION

To Grandma Finch

ACKNOWLEDGMENTS

Thank you Jerrod S. Smelker, Dad, for helping me along the way to writing my first book. Without you, I would have only flailed about helplessly.

Thanks to Mr. Branch, who brought my English skills back into fruition, and who always knew I could make things happen.

Thanks to Zynt Ford, Ollie Froelich, and Zander Noah, my best friends whom I would be a goner without.

HELLSTITCHER

Prologue

Silence filled the air like a noxious gas cloud, surrounding anything in its vicinity. In a room of immaculate and beautiful darkness, lit only by the dim lamp on the coffee table, one man, the famed star actor, Ben Hoves, sat on his lovely leather couch. He was still wearing his gorgeous tuxedo suit, most definitely from a fancy gathering earlier in the day, bound by ropes. I knew it was his time to go.

On the coffee table, the cheap lamp was not alone; there also rested a hunting knife. The lamp stood at a measly two feet tall and screamed "cheapskate" at everyone who looked at it. The blade looked to be around six inches long and an enormous two inches wide. It's enough to slice anyone apart in a matter of seconds. The metal looked to be carbon-colored and polished; its darkness held more history than an old one-room schoolhouse. Its colossal body had a curved rear end with designs etched into the metal, enhancing the blade's personality even more. This weapon...was a messmaker.

Hoves woke up, unaware of the doom that would soon be upon him. He's just now realizing his body was in binds, strapped to his couch. He started to panic and began shaking. His grunts of fear were like a beautiful melody.

"Hello? Linda? Can you hear me?" he yelled.

I grinned. What entertainment it was to watch the worst-feared death. It didn't happen very often when I got my contracts. I knew it was so close, but I could not contain my excitement for much longer. I wanted to see blood; I wanted to see death fall upon this useless man! Finally, I spoke.

"Do you know why you're here, Mr. Hoves?" I asked.

The man still squirmed in his binds, clearly trying to break out of it and escape the area. He didn't hear me at all. If he did, I'd be the one caught off guard. Sweat dripped from his short brown hair and down to his head. A drop landed on his circular glasses, urging him to try and shake it off the lens, to no avail. His face was turning to a shade of vermillion, but the lamp's pathetic lighting did a fair job at concealing it, however.

"Help! Someone! Someone hear me! I can't break free! Please!" he kept screaming out.

Hoves started gasping out of his panic, as if it would help him relax. Relaxing was the last thing I'd expect to see him do in his predicament. Though it didn't appear he would relax anytime soon.

"Your time has come, Mr. Hoves. Someone out in the vast world hated you so much they were willing to sell their own soul to know you were dead. That is why you're here," I told him, knowing he still couldn't hear me.

He started to cry and continued to yell for his wife. "Linda! Help! Linda! Where are you when I need you?!"

Tears streamed down his terrorized face like a flowing, carving river, much to my pleasure. I began to laugh, harder and harder. I had to settle down so I could continue watching. Something had to happen soon…!

I knew what to do; I didn't know if I'd be able to hold my laughter in after this, but hell, it'd be worth it.

"Right, that's my mistake!" I started. "It slipped my mind. I forgot you couldn't hear me."

I took a Sulfric Growler from my satchel and held it in between my fingers. This small capsule was made by the Devil himself, in case we wanted to entertain ourselves. The job got boring often times, and a little bit of fun could go a long way.

I crushed the capsule between my thumb and forefinger right under his nose. His face went from fear to disgust in a matter of seconds, now smelling the foul stench of the odorous powder.

He refocused his sight, and we locked eyes.

He started screaming again, this time unintelligible words. The tears came faster, and his shaking became violent. I genuinely thought for a moment that he might just suffer a heart attack. I started laughing again, much harder than earlier.

"Stop! Stop! Stop! Please don't kill me!" he cried out. "I don't deserve to die! I'm only thirty! I… Help! Linda!"

Once again, I had to force myself out of laughter. This was too good! It'd been so long since I had a fun contract!

"She cannot help you! No one can!" I yelled. "Your death is here, at last! I am enjoying this far more than I had imagined I would!"

"Why?! Why?!" He sobbed. "I don't wanna die! What did I do?! I never… I never… This wasn't supposed to be how my life went!"

"Of course not!" I replied. "It wasn't up to you,

nor me. You will die because someone sold their soul to have you killed! That's why I'm here. It's why you are here. Who could have hated you so much that they'd sacrifice their own soul just to see you die?"

He turned pale and went silent. He rotated his head to the side to show himself thinking. I could see every pore on his small face from this angle. He made a hard gulping noise and stuttered, "I— I— What d-do you mean? I never...wronged anyone," he started and slowly hung his head low in defeat. "Who could ever... I don't... I don't understand."

I put my large yellow hand on his shoulder, covering almost half of his entire arm's sleeve. The incandescence from my forearm lit up his body ever so slightly. I sighed and pretended to sound sincere.

"It must be hard being in this situation. I don't understand your pain nor feel bad for you, but I do hope the best for your soul once it moves on. You will die a death most fearful, by your standards." I sighed once again and paused. I looked to the floor for a moment, then back at Hoves. "Mr. Hoves, I destroyed your family heirloom. I felt you needed to know that before you went. It was quite the work of art, I'll admit. Oh well."

Mr. Hoves gave me a face of confusion. He had no idea how in the world his heirloom was important to his death. I did. I did know how important it was. It perhaps was the most important aspect of this entire endeavor.

I took a step back to observe the scene once again. Hoves had just noticed the blade, and he started crying again. I smiled at his attempts to free himself from the binds of his sins. The ropes were obviously knotted taut; I assumed it was because of how skinny Mr. Hoves was. His body looked like it hadn't eaten for days or even weeks. A man like him could easily slip away from being bound to the couch if the rigger was careless enough.

"What are you going to do to me? Just take me out quickly! Don't make it painful. Just kill me already if you're going to!" he yelled at me.

"I'm not going to kill you!" I yelled back. "I am simply going to observe and bask in amazement."

Hoves drew an angry expression on his face and started to squirm more and more, desperate to escape his fate. The lines on his face told stories of stress in his young age, and in his struggle to cope with death, they just grew.

His body went limp for a moment, his head hitting the back cushion of his couch, slightly messing up his hair. His eyes were closed, and his rapid breathing began to slow down. He stayed this way for what seemed like thirty minutes, although my less-than-acute sense of time told me it had only been thirty seconds.

Finally, after what seemed like hours, as the sweaty man gathered his final thoughts within the last few moments of his life, a little boy walked into the light. Curiosity struck me like a bolt of lightning; I wondered just what would happen next. This boy looked to be no older than seven and no taller than four feet six inches. His hair looked to be a dirty-blond color, but the lamp still betrayed my eyesight.

Hoves seemed to notice his presence, refocusing his attention to the child. No doubt, this kid was Hoves' son. There'd be no other explanation for him to be here with us.

"Markus! Markus! Hey, buddy!" Hoves said, his ugly face turning excited. "Hey, Daddy's in a bit of a bind right now. Can you help me?"

The child did nothing. He *said* nothing. He stared. He stared into his father's blue eyes. His blank pupils betrayed his consciousness. There were no thoughts inside of his thick head; I could tell. This was it. This was how Hoves died.

Markus continued to stare, and the longer he waited, the more confused the father looked. The confusion slowly turned into worry, and the worry slowly turned into realization.

"Markus, buddy, you need to untie me. Right now," Hoves firmly told his son.

Though the father had given his son an order, the boy had yet to move. Hoves seemed to grow angry, and he continued to egg his son on.

"Markus! Untie me. Hey, do you wanna play catch again today? We can do that, but you have to get me out of here. Take the knife, be careful, but cut me out! Now!" he said while raising his voice.

Markus made a move. Slowly, he turned his stare down to the deadly knife that lay on the coffee table. Moments passed, as Hoves' face grew more and more worried.

The child reached for the knife and gently picked it up off the wooden table. He continued to stare at it, still without any sign of conscience. He then looked back at his father and started to approach him, ever so slowly.

"Markus, buddy, I need you to cut me loose, all right? Do you understand?" Hoves pleaded. "You need to break Daddy out of here."

Markus stopped a foot in front of the sweating adult, where the figure stood straight and expressionless. He put his index finger to his lips.

"Shhhh..." he whispered, eerily. He was quiet as a mouse. If the room wasn't already soundless, nobody would have been able to hear him.

"Markus! Cut me loose! Now! Don't just stand there!" Hoves began to yell, angrily. "Can't you see that monster? He says I'm going to die! Help me, Markus!"

Hoves once again swapped faces, going from angry to despair in a matter of seconds as his son raised the knife to Hoves' head, still silent. This adult man would be killed by his own son, I knew for sure. Normal contracts were purely snooze fests; the majority of victims would only have their organs incinerated. It's no fun at all, but this, this was like watching an opera. Its beauty and magnificence was almost too much to handle.

Markus spoke once more. "See no evil."

As he said this, he slammed his father's head to the cushion. It knocked the glasses off of Hoves' moist face and messed up his hair even more. Markus positioned the knife to the eyeballs and slit them open, blood gushing out like a jelly-filled doughnut. The screams were ear-piercing, his vocals going past the limit of what should be possible. I started to laugh again. This was a show I'd pay for!

"Hear no evil!" Markus said, this time yelling. He wasted no time after maliciously lacerating his dad's eyes.

He violently grabbed his dad's head and started sawing at the left ear. Hoves' legs, arms, and whole body was shaking rapidly; a storm had whipped up, and it targeted his nervous system. The ear fell off, and with it, a river of blood spewed from the wound. Markus began hacking away at the right ear, more quickly than the first.

"MARKUS! MARKUS! STOP! STOP! MARKUS!" Hoves screamed. He repeated this until the other ear had been detached from his head, then only screamed pain.

"Speak no evil!" Markus yelled again. The heavy flow of blood was piercing my nostrils at this point. Its aroma certainly replaced the smell of fancy new furniture, as all wealthy humans had. One whiff of the oncoming death was almost like a drug to me.

This time he clenched his hand into a fist and rapid-fired it into the man's nose, breaking it. For a split second, this stunned Hoves, and the boy crammed his hand in his dad's open mouth. Hoves didn't react in time, and Markus snatched the tongue. Fast as lightning, he yanked it out and sliced it clean off. The amount of blood that followed was uncanny. It was absurd. It was horrendous. It was sickening. Yet it made me enjoy it that much more.

As I laughed louder, Hoves sat with a blood-curdling screech flying from his bleeding mouth. The screams paused, and they were replaced with choking. He threw up globs of blood and started suffocating. I laughed harder! What a graceful sequence of events! So atrocious, yet so hilarious.

Hoves continued to desperately cling onto life, gurgling blood disgustingly. He tried to grab the leather cushions, but his fingers were too weak. He started to slump and threw his head to the sky. Hoves' chest kept rising rapidly but quickly burned out and faded away into the ice-cold depths of the sea. It rose for the last time and lowered like a fire dying with the wind.

Seconds passed, and Markus was still staring at the body of Ben Hoves, breathing heavily. My laughter faded, but the smile on my face stayed. Markus suddenly dropped the knife and stared wide eyed at his father's mutilated corpse.

"Daddy?" the boy whimpered. His face turned red, and his own bright blue eyes watered up. Tears were beginning to drop like bullets. I almost began to laugh again.

"Daddy?" Markus repeated, crying. He got close up to the dead body's head. He started wailing. He had no idea what atrocity he had just committed.

Yes...how graceful.

Chapter One

Hate

"Decipere!"

My eyes opened, and I looked up. Towering above me was the fallen angel, the Devil himself. The average human couldn't comprehend the sheer, unfathomable size of this demon. His body was a skyscraper and mine an ant.

The Devil looked down upon me with a red face. Glaring eyes seized my heart, yet I could only feel rage. Him being above me put my mind in a state of constant unrest. It was not right! Why was he the one in charge, when all he did was sit around on that colossal throne and watch the demons fly by? He didn't show any sort of care about his own home. Hell was a mess.

Of all the things I could have been made into, I was made a Hellstitcher. I was no Devil or God, so why even put me in this plane of existence? Why had I been put in this wretched horror story? If I could not be the very best, there wasn't even a point to being here.

"Decipere! I am speaking to you!" he roared. His deep voice echoed within the trenches of Hell; it was heard from every corner.

"What is it you need, sire?" I replied, kneeling to

the ground. This pathetic position should be the other way around. He should be the one kneeling, not me! How could he treat me, Decipere, Monger of the Hellstitchers, as some sort of rat, as some sort of disgusting animal, needing to be put down?

"You are wasting my time and patience. Are you not done with your contract?!" Satan yelled. "It's been two whole days since you received it, and all you've been doing is moping around Hell!"

"I have not been moping!" I yelled back, furious at his accusations. "I have simply been busy, and this contract is making me fall asleep just thinking about it. It's just a boring man who wants another boring man dead because these boring men have boring family issues. None of it entertains me in the slightest. Besides, I'm out of Sulfric Growlers. You know I'm not going to prioritize the contract without them."

I lied to him. The contract was not a single bit boring. All I had in mind was getting more capsules, as I had truthfully run out. The problem was that asking Satan for more capsules for the second time in a month was asking to get slapped in the face and spat on. It's atrocious how he treated these like an addicting drug, when in reality they're one of my only forms of amusement. I wouldn't go into more than one contract at a time without having them.

"Do you think that it matters to me whether you enjoy it or not?" Satan replied. "You do this because there is nothing else you can do. It is your purpose. I only give you the Sulfric Growlers because the thought of humans seeing you amuses me. You make your own entertainment; it is neither my job nor my problem."

I only stared at his monstrous head angrily. The

lava streaming from Satan's arms was flowing faster than normal, meaning he's just in a worse mood. I considered yelling back at him and demanding more capsules, but he might simply end up taking them away permanently.

"Fine," I growled, face twitching. "I'll finish my contract, but the next one has to be somewhat interesting."

"Good," he said back. "Make it fast. Tenebris is the only Hellstitcher I have available. If we get another contract, we could miss the next one. You know that cannot happen, Decipere."

"Tell Tenebris no one wants him as a Hellstitcher anyway," I blurted out. "That mongrel won't even have a chance to get another contract before I receive my next one."

I wasn't sure about that. It could absolutely happen, but now that I'd said it, I was going to make sure it didn't. Tenebris was a lousy Hellstitcher, always talking too much, always boasting about his skill, never shutting his lips about being the "best." He did his job, I supposed, but it was never as clean a job as mine. I was the best of the Hellstitchers, after all. He was the worst.

Lucifer bent down and shrank his size. Starting from being a big, red behemoth, he slowly lost his mass and sized himself down to his conversational appearance. Almost only twice the height of me now, he steadily approached my person with a settled expression on his face. Once he reached my location, he lifted his hand and placed it on my stony shoulder. Patient lava oozed out of it, and I felt the heat all throughout my body. I donned a slight sense of fear, curious as to what he was trying to do. This smaller form of him was always somehow…intimidating. I kept a straight face so as to not show my anxiety.

"Just. Finish. The contract," he whispered, looking sincere. And out of nowhere, he shrieked, "NOW!!"

My body jumped, and I looked down. This was utterly humiliating.

Satan's expression stayed at a fixed state of malice as he slowly turned away and then walked back to his throne. He grew his body back to its full size, now keeping that form. He took a seat in his throne and continued to glare at my wretched mind.

"Or else," he finished.

I was so unbelievably pissed off. I could have ripped a whale in half, if given the chance. Treated like scum yet again. That's something that'd never change, unless something extraordinary appeared at my feet. I wanted to kill him. I wanted to be the one to rip his innards out. I wanted to look him in the eyes and say, "Eat it!" right before dealing the final blow.

I turned around and began walking away, groaning. I headed to my bloodportal: my only way in or out of Hell. If one wanted, they could open a portal outside of Hell, to the gates. That would be foolish, however. Cerberus guarded the gates like a mother bear guarded her cub. I'd never seen Cerberus before, but he'd been told to maul even the ones who accidentally strayed too close to the gates. It didn't matter if they didn't want to break in; they got too close, therefore they would be punished.

I plunged my large hands into the crying bloodportal's opening and grasped the sides. With a slight grunt, I forced it open and stepped inside. The doorway was entirely bathed in blood, flowing around every which way.

My destination was a place called Canada. My current target was a man who thought of himself as the protagonist of the game of life. So petty, so greedy, and so narcissistic. Allegedly, he kicked his brother out of his house after the brother realized he'd been sleeping with all sorts of prostitutes and was having an affair with his wife. The brother was going to inform the wife but never got the chance to, as he was attacked ruthlessly and was left out to fend for himself. Leaving that man on the streets for weeks on end turned him even more bitter and resentful. That brother was my contractor.

Although it's none of my business, and quite honestly not anything I truly cared about, I was still always curious about the reasoning behind calling upon the help of the Hellstitchers. Most of the time, it was pointless anger and hatred toward someone else who did them wrong only a single time. Sometimes, however, it was a reason that made me question my own decision-making. A girl, fifteen years ago, once received my help. She wanted a certain somebody to die because of his evolution from a loving man into a corrupt political figure. One of the world's most famous, by far.

That contract's reasoning wasn't why I had trouble with my own actions, however. The man she spoke of turned out to be only a puppet for a man of even higher status to play with. Witnessing everything that happened with that contract made me doubt my own intentions. It made me wonder if I was being played with by the Devil. He could be using me as a tool, as a means to gain even more power. The only power he could ever gain was the authority over God himself...but that just wasn't possible. It wasn't supposed to be, at least.

It also made me wonder if I could toy with others as well. If I could...use them and make them mine, I could slowly reign supreme over whomever I wanted...although that wasn't what I truly wanted. What I wanted, what I believed I had the potential to be, was the absolute ruler of Hell. It just had to be me. The Devil wasn't good enough...always lazy and uncaring. I felt entitled to that position, but there was simply no way of achieving it. Not right now, at least. Using others as my own personal play toy was just a small aspect of going for the gold. Not moral in the slightest, but incredibly useful and effective. Besides, it's not like it'd kill them. They could get angry all they wanted, but they'd get over it with time.

As my foot stepped through the portal, my rocky and molten skin grew cold, and in a moment, I was on Earth. The bright daylight seared my eyes, so much so that I winced in pain. I quickly regained my focus and put my muscular arm above my eyes. That's when I realized the portal took me to where I was before I left Earth: to the brick house of Joey Sunders.

I jumped down to the ground, onto the empty sidewalk, littered with used soda cans and grocery bags. I felt a wet sensation on my foot, and I saw that I'd landed in a small puddle of rainwater. I took a step in the grass, realizing it, too, was soaked in rain. The clouds above me weren't pouring water onto me, but they were as heavy and gray as a ball of lead.

One thing I always did before I struck my victims was stalk them for a day, watching them, silent as could be. It was part of the fun. Or that's what I tried to tell myself. It was really just exhausting, watching a human go about their normal life. It's always sleep inducing. I did this to get an idea of who they were and what they were like. The interactions they made with others and the actions they performed by themselves meant quite a lot to me. After learning who they were, they often gave me an idea of how I needed to go about finding the things they held close to them. Objects, people, beliefs, and places. It all could work, but only the objects were allowed to burn.

Joey Sunders was already someone I'd stalked. Back when I got my contract on him, I watched him sleep with more prostitutes and continue to evade his wife's eyes of a hawk. He performed exceptionally well at keeping his secret hidden. Going as far as to create a fake back in his closet to hide his guests when the wife came home was impressive. I'd never seen anyone be so desperate to be sleazy, and it was utterly horrid. How could someone lust so viciously for other humans that they went and turned their back on the ones who loved them?

The only objective I had at the moment was finding something emotionally valuable to him. If I had to take a guess, it'd be his bank account. Of course, I couldn't physically destroy something like that. Perhaps, though, I could destroy his entire wallet. I wasn't sure if that's worth a try, but it could work out in my favor. If he came home and couldn't find his wallet or his cash, he could cause a chain reaction leading to violence from his own end. Satan certainly wouldn't want that to happen. But then again...considering he *would* resort to such aggression in order to find his money, it'd make sense to believe he indeed had some kind of attachment to it. If this didn't work out, I would have to take another big look around his room, finding an alternative relatively quickly.

Wind howled to the sky as I began to stride toward Sunders' house. The cool breeze felt relaxing on my muscular, rocky body. My horns ran against the wind, giving me a heroic sensation. When I finally reached the door, I didn't have to knock or turn the knob. I let focus take me by the hand, and as a ghostly apparition, I walked straight through the solid wood door.

A stench of garbage and beer stung my nostrils as I first came inside, its potency sharp as a needle. The smell from the stalking session I had differentiated from this by a notable margin. My senses were keen as a wolf, but at times like this, I wished that they were not. Crashed down on the hardwood floor, next to the fur couch, was Sunders himself. His long blond hair was in a rat's nest, and his shirt was nearly ripped in half. A broken bottle of half-spilled beer lay beside his hand. This was a shameful way to live.

I took a large step over Sunders' body, carefully avoiding touching him. If that heinous man ever laid a finger on me, I'd snap his throat in an instant. My foot stepped on the foot of another party animal I didn't notice, this time a druggie with a syringe still hanging from his forearm. His clothes were all taken off, save for his undergarments. I let out a gag and immediately jumped off of it.

As swift as I could be, I rushed to the bedroom of the house, cautiously avoiding all the other disgusting scumbags. I counted six in total, all of them knocked out cold. If this was how Sunders got caught by his wife, he'd be dead before I could get to him.

Once again, I phased through the bedroom door so as to not make any noise that could wake up the druggies. Inside the master bedroom, there lay a large, king-sized bed, with the white sheets all over the floor. No one was in the room, but the putrid scent followed. A stain of alcohol purged the wall to my right, and the shattered remains of a glass bottle rested below it. I turned to the nightstand and took one big step toward it. I had to move the glass lamp onto the bed before I could start digging, but that was hardly an issue.

I started rummaging through the articles of trash on top of the nightstand. The wallet had to be there somewhere; it's where I saw him leave it last. Granted, it'd been two days since I'd been here, but there's still a chance. More and more pieces of worthless junk came into my large hands, but I still didn't find the wallet. I tossed the junk onto the bed along with the lamp, most of it finding its way onto the floor instead.

Only a few seconds later, I emptied the nightstand completely. There was no wallet to be found. I had to look somewhere else.

"Augh!" I yelled in frustration. I tightened my grip on the nightstand, wanting to smash it to bits. Doing that wouldn't help me any, however. I could tell the extensive heat from my arms was affecting its metal, though. On the spots where my hands gripped it, the metal seemed to slightly melt away and bend the nightstand over.

I rolled my eyes and continued my search. Minutes and minutes of opening drawers, tossing trash onto the bed, and lifting furniture added more wasted time to my efforts. The wallet was not in this room.

Phasing back into the hallway leading to the living room, I began my search again. I rummaged through the wooden cupboards, drawers, and containers scattered around the house. My efforts continued to bear no fruit, as the wallet was still nowhere to be found. As each second passed, I felt myself growing more and more impatient.

I decided to take a break for a few minutes. Perhaps I could come up with some ideas while I relaxed. I walked over to the fur couch, already have searching between its cushions, and sat down with a sigh. I'd checked and double checked every container I could get my hands on, and I'd scoured the entire house just for this little wallet. I may have to find another item to destroy, but with all the debris laying around, it's difficult to pinpoint what Sunders truly cared about.

Then a realization struck me. Sunders... He may be the key. If there was no place in his home that the wallet was, then surely it could be with him?

I got up at once, locking my sights onto Sunders' body, still blacked out. I leaped over the couch and landed with a loud crash. Within moments, I was on the ground, sticking my finger into his pockets. I felt a small object touch my fingertip, and the texture reeked of leather.

I snatched the treasure out of his pocket and

held it up to my eyes. The wallet was mine! I laughed in my victory and proceeded to crush the wallet immediately. It burned like hellfire, and without any trace of its existence, the wallet had been incinerated. A black cloud of dust erupted from my hands, followed by a faint screech, letting me know I'd chosen the right item.

I laughed some more, pointing at Sunders.

"Haha! You lose, Sunders!" I yelled aloud. "How does it feel to have your fate sealed? Do you feel sad? Does it hurt? Show me where it hurts. I'll bruise it some more!" I continued to berate the unconscious body without any hesitation and with the utmost celebration. Smoke not seeping from his mouth told me it was going to be another fun-filled death!

I waited. Smiling, I looked forward to witnessing bloodshed take place unto this atrocity of a man. What could Sunders possibly fear most? Maybe his wife? Maybe a car crash? Maybe an animal? So many options, so many possibilities, but only one answer.

Hours passed, but I continued to watch the sleeping man. Sitting around for a death like this was worth all of the waiting; it was the only time I could watch life erode. Not being allowed to outright murder the victims myself was equal to a prison sentence for me. My history with combat and death matches gave me an overwhelming urge to kill, and my status of being the Monger only told me I was the very best at it.

After what felt like an eternity, the man finally moved. He groaned and clutched his stomach as he tried to get up. He put another hand on his forehead, likely having a migraine from his hangover. He trudged through the house, aimlessly wandering toward nowhere. I was curious as to what was going on, not knowing if this was a part of his execution.

Another man woke up, yelling as he got up. Incomprehensible words shot out of his mouth, as he, too, was suffering a hangover. Eventually, Sunders found his way to the other man. He looked upset and started shouting at him.

"George, you idiot! I told you only one drink!" Sunders cried. "Look what you did to my house, you bastard!"

George looked at him without a thought between his eyes, unable to process what was just laid onto him. He lifted a finger up, while slouching his body, and simply threw it at the ground. Sunders wasn't waiting around, as he threw a fist into George's jaw, knocking him back onto the ground. I got closer, beaming as I watched the future unfold.

"What the fuck, Joe!" George yelled, finally getting a grip onto reality. "What was that for?"

"You stupid drunkard. My house is a mess, and it's all your fault!" Joey fired back.

"I didn't do nothing, Joey! You're the one who wanted to bring drinks. Why am I being blamed?"

"You wanted me to have one more shot! You told me one more! And one more after another, my decision making was gone! I don't even remember how many we had!" Joey yelled, enraged at his companion. Clearly, the problem came from Joey, giving in to the pleasure of drinking once again.

"You're overreacting. I never said nothing like that!" George argued. "It's not like your decision-making was perfect in the first place. Don't act like you're the innocent one here. If you didn't want me to bring drinks, your house might still be a decent place to live."

"What did you say?! Are you saying my house is a junkyard?! Answer me, asshole! My house is perfectly fine!"

"Yeah, maybe I am saying that. Whaddaya gonna do about it? It's true, and you know it."

Joey didn't say anything back but only screamed and ran to the kitchen. George used the opportunity to stand up and shake his head at the rampaging man. He ran a hand over his bald head and let out a sigh. Joey's screams were becoming closer again as he burst through the hallway with a butcher knife in hand.

George's eyes went wide, and he attempted to flee, but Sunders got ahold of his shirt and clung onto him like a leech. Sunders tried taking a swing at George's neck, but George ducked milliseconds before the blade reached him. He recovered fast and got ahold of Sunders' arm. With little effort, George had yanked him into the air.

George's large size and strength allowed him to launch Sunders an incredible distance, smashing him into the expensive TV stand. The enormous flat-screen TV sitting at the top wobbled around, as it was only held up by the uneven wooden stand clearly not made to carry such weight. Joey attempted to get up, but George had already made his way over to him.

With one big kick, Joey was sent once again into the TV stand, this time with much greater force. My eyes were glued to the fight, not wanting to miss a single second of it. The hefty TV wobbled once again, getting even closer to the edge. The butcher knife was on the ground, only a few feet away from Sunders. He glanced at it and looked to George.

"Don't you even think about it, Joe!" George bellowed.

Joey did think about it, and surely, he didn't think of anything else. He leaped for the knife, his body weakened. He was too late, for George wasn't injured nearly as much. He was picked up once again, and George shot him toward the stand for the final time.

Joey had only a second to regain focus and look to the sky. There, the flat-screen was bolting down to the ground, and in its path was Joey Sunders. An ear-piercing *splat* came from the collision, marking my contract over with.

Laughter burst out from my mouth. Joey was dead! And his own buddy got him killed! Crushed by a giant TV, what a way to go out. His greatest fear had to be getting mashed, no doubt, but having it done by a TV was pure humiliation. It was like a mark of punishment, being smashed by your own symbol of wealth.

George was still watching the dead body as he had realized what his actions caused. He put a trembling hand to his gaping mouth and started breathing irregularly. Tears began to stream from his eyes, not knowing what to do.

"O-oh my...oh my...oh...no, wha...why..." he muttered in a whisper.

People had already woken up from the sound of fighting, and one girl managed to make her way over to the scene. A decibel-defying shriek followed, alarming everyone in the state.

My laughter faded, and I decided it would be an ideal time to leave. Making my way through the house, I once again had to be cautious not to touch the now-awake druggies. As soon as I was clear of obstacles, I rushed to the door and phased out of it.

The cold wind whistled against my body, and rain trickled down from the sky. As the rainwater sizzled against the yellow sections of my skin, I began opening my bloodportal before the rain became too much to bear. This portal would take me to the house of Dean Morris, the one signing the contract. Reporting Sunders' death to him was my last chore.

Once I stepped inside, I was greeted with another scent, this time much sweeter and more beautiful. Morris' house was almost the opposite of Sunders', cleanliness speaking.

Morris was already in the room, reading a book at his one-seater dining table. He noticed my presence immediately and stood up at the speed of light.

"Well, Hellstitcher, is he dead? He's dead, right? That's why you're here?" he asked frantically.

"Shut up, human," I deflected. "You have no reason to speak, only to listen."

I paused for a moment, waiting to get a response from Morris so that I could yell at him again. His breathing was erratic, clearly due to the nervousness of being face-to-face with a Hellstitcher.

"I-I, okay, sure—" he started.

"I told you to shut up!" I screamed, moving closer to him. I wasn't angry in the slightest, but instilling fear into anyone I could was what I did. It let them know I was in charge and that what I said went. It let them know they were weak.

"Sunders is dead," I began. "And with it, your soul is also dead. It belongs to the Devil now. Hehehe... I hope you enjoy an infinite cycle of torment."

Morris' face grew pale, and he sat back down, avoiding eye contact. His hands gripped his knees and clawed at them. He shook his head up and down, understanding his destiny. He took deep breaths and turned back to his wrinkled book.

I let out a chuckle and slowly walked away, back to my bloodportal. My contract had been completed.

Chapter Two

Love

"Daddy!"

I lost my train of thought and looked up from my computer. Standing in front of my desk was the only love I had: my daughter. A mile-long smile covered her face as she awaited my response.

I smiled at her, cherishing her own smile. My daughter was the only one I lived for. Her future was what mattered most to me; with her gone, it's as if I was gone, too. I'd do anything and everything to make sure she got a life worth living. That was why I was working on a project that only I could complete.

"Yes, Munchkin?" I said back to her.

"Look, I made this for you!" she yelled, holding up her handiwork. It was an ornament of sticks and glue, held together in the shape of two stickmen. One was half the size of the other and holding the bigger one's hand. "It's me and you. Do you like it?" she asked innocently.

"Oh, Lila," I replied, getting out of my chair and walking to my daughter. I kneeled down to her size and continued. "This is gorgeous. I didn't know you could make such a fantastic work of art."

I held the sculpture in my hand and looked it over, gleaming at it. She loved to make me little crafts once in a while, and I kept every one of them. Anything she could get her hands on, she'd try and turn it into a symbol of her love. It was sweet. Even if it meant my work schedule getting ripped in half, I was always happy to receive them. A child's imagination and their work to realize it were priceless; they shouldn't ever be ignored.

"Thank you, Daddy!" Lila said. She turned away and skipped out of the room within a matter of seconds. Off to go back to playing with her toys, I'd imagine. She didn't have much more to do in my house...

My wife, Marie, passed away at Lila's birth. She was the strongest soldier I had ever met...but childbirth was too much for her aged body to handle. Marie and I had been together for thirty years but had never had children until Lila. Now I was a granddad-aged father with a single child. Some may say it's unfortunate, but I saw it only as a blessing.

My parents were also both deceased. My father was never a part of my life, but my mother told me that he was a scumbag, a nobody who never even deserved to breathe. Something like that was not ever how she would describe any person, save for him. My mother was a religious woman, a Christian like no other. She would never say anything vicious of others. When she passed away, Marie was the only one who I lived for, but now that both my parents and my wife were gone, the only one who deserved my attention was my beloved daughter.

If only I had more time in my life to be her father, I'd be a happier man and she a happier kid. At sixty-five years of age, I didn't have very long. I should have retired by now, but the expenses in my big project had kept me away from retirement. As a man of science, the resources needed to run experiments and tests added up to a sizable sum of cash. The good news about this was that the project was almost complete, and after it's done, I could safely earn enough money to retire within a few years. Not many years of retirement lay ahead, but this project was my life's work, and I'd have it finished, even if it's the last thing I did.

I got back up and walked back to my desk. I stared at my computer monitor for a moment and plopped back down on my leather swivel chair. The screen showed a pie chart of different outcomes for tests. These were for my coworkers back at the lab; I had to have this done by the end of the week. Despite only having one more day to complete it after tonight, I shut off the computer and closed my eyes.

I thought, and thought, and thought, and thought. I let out a sigh and threw my head back. My project required the next step to be completed soon, very soon. I wasn't ready to begin yet, but I was confident the scene could still be set in motion. All I needed was Gomez's permission before he left. That's only three days away. If I could get him to perform the ritual, I would finally be able to put my project to rest. The Hellstitchers would terrorize no one after I was done with this.

I opened my eyes and quickly snatched my cell phone from my lab pocket. I dialed in Gomez's number and let it ring. My mouth tensed up as I listened to the ringing, and my heart pounded harder and harder.

Not even five seconds later, the phone picked up. Gomez greeted me and attempted to get a stab at small talk, but I hastily deflected it.

"Gomez, look, uh, this isn't the time for discussing last night's supper. I really need...uh... I-It's time, Gomez," I told him, scratching my legs. My leg was bouncing, too, jumping up and down to a trampoline playing in my head.

"Buddy, look... I, eh... I already told you; it shouldn't be anything you're doing business with. Why can't you leave it alone?" Gomez argued back.

"You know why. Come on, I don't have anyone else who'd be willing to do it. Plus, you know that once I win, your soul won't be sent to Hell," I replied, getting desperate. This was my last shot at getting what I needed. If Gomez wouldn't do it, there wasn't anyone else I trusted who would.

"How do you know that, Doc? You're a smart guy and all, but this isn't really your field of expertise. I mean, for all I know, your mother could have just been a whack job, and you're playing into her game. The Hellstitchers probably can't be killed by the likes of us anyway."

"My mother was no whack job, I can assure you. Please, Gomez, you know this is the only chance I have at this. My life's work can't be done in vain."

Gomez sighed and paused. Eventually, he spoke again.

"The cost is my soul... If you mess this up, I could be damned to an eternal inferno," he said quietly.

"I know that. That's why I can only ask you. You're the one I trust, and you trust me. I've worked on this for forty long years. I don't think there's any way I can mess it up. I need you to put all of your trust in me. If you can do that, I can deliver results. Positive results."

Another pause came from him, this time longer than the first. I waited in agony, craving his answer more and more. Scratches on my leg sped up, and as did the leg bouncing.

"If I do this, I'll have your word that...that you'll succeed in...in killing them?" he asked.

"Of course, of course!" I blurted out. "You'll have my absolute word. Count on it."

"Yeah...okay. Okay...okay, I'll do it for you...I guess. Just, eh... I'll perform the ritual Saturday morning. That'll be the night before I leave the state. I'll be living on the road after that. Roaming the country...that's all I've ever dreamed of. G—"

"Oh, thank you, thank you, Gomez!" I said excitedly, cutting him off. "Seriously, this means more to me than you know. Next time I call you, it'll be letting you know your soul is safe, all right?"

"'Course. Don't let me end up like Tony..." he said, abruptly hanging up afterward.

I let out a sigh of relief and put my hand over my silver, boxed beard. I let my hand go limp and smiled at the ceiling. In two days' time, I'd have a Hellstitcher tailing me. They wouldn't be able to kill me, no matter how hard they tried, many thanks to their rules of assassinating.

Tony was another friend of mine. We'd tried to experiment with the Hellstitchers before, to gain valuable information. What we gained was not worth the sacrifice we accidentally took, claiming only a demonic weapon and blood on our hands. Sure, we got some information, but it would have only been useful before we performed the ritual. The endeavor was not something we took lightly; Tony was gone, and so was our chance at getting more information from the Hellstitcher he called. Gomez quit right on the spot, but I wasn't going to let the sacrifice go in vain. I'd been working on my own since then.

My phone rang again, shutting down my brief moment of satisfaction. I picked up my phone to realize Gomez was calling again. Confused, I stared for a second before clicking "answer." If he was calling me again, it would have to be about my plan, no doubt. Although he didn't know much about it, I guessed he deserved to know.

"Hey, you okay?" I answered.

"Yeah, yeah... It's just..." he started, taking in a deep breath. "I don't know. I feel like if I'm really selling my soul, I should help out more, ya know? Like, I want to make sure your plans get carried out, so I don't get sentenced to the lake of fire. I have to make sure."

"Yes, of course. It means a lot that you want to help out more. However, I don't know of any way you can. I have everything prepared already. All you can do is wait."

Not everything was prepared, but I couldn't let him know that. He could back out any time he wanted, and I'd be stuck. All that needed to be done was finishing the weapon. That's all I needed. My time was running out, but I knew I could complete it within the time limit.

"C'mon, there isn't anything I can do? Can't I— *scoff*—at least watch? Give you some backup in case things go south? You're the only one who's working to do something about these things. I can't just wait for something to happen."

I considered what he said for a moment, trying to come up with some possible solution. Alas, nothing came to my mind; my brain blanked completely. The absurd silence that protruded from my mouth already gave him my answer, but he still waited. No solution was clear, but what could I do?

"Yeah..." he started again. "I get it. What use can I even be to you? You're the scientist; you're the doctor. I'm retired, I'm just... You know what? I couldn't even watch if I tried. Opal and I aren't going to see you for months, maybe years. The most I could do is check up on you. But what am I supposed to do if you end up dead? What then? Wh—"

"I won't end up dead!" I yelled, interrupting him. "Gomez...the only thing you can do is just... You have to trust me. We've been partners for fifty years, and you know I always do what I say. You know this. We both know this. I have everything I need to kill the Hellstitchers, and I'm the only one who knows how to, and who's willing to, pull it off."

Gomez was silent. Nothing came from his end, not a single sound. At first, I assumed the call was being buggy, and I prepared myself to repeat his name. Before I could speak, however, Gomez began to mutter. I couldn't understand what he was trying to say to me, but I let it go on. He may have been interrupted by his wife or by another disturbance. I patiently waited for his voice to morph into clear words again.

"I gotta go, sorry," he piped. "Listen, this could seal both of our fates. If you mess this up...I don't know how you're supposed to fix it."

"I understand," I said quietly. "Thanks, Gomez."

"Yeah," he muttered again before hanging up for the second time. Gomez didn't deserve to be put in this position, and neither did I. Parts of me wished that this job would have fallen on someone else's hands, but if it was up to someone who did deserve it, I'd have to assume they wouldn't follow through.

I slapped my cell phone down on my desk, face down. This was going to work. I was going to kill the Hellstitchers, and there's not a damn thing they could do to stop me. Whatever lay ahead of me on my path would be conquered. I had everything I needed, and once my weapon was completed, my slaughter would be repentless. They deserved it; those vile beings of darkness had been killing for who knew how long, and at last, someone had the power to end it all.

I stood up and placed the glasses back on my head. I slowly walked out of the door and into my living room, where my daughter was drawing on her miniature canvas. It appeared to be a bear, donning a top hat and a bow tie. I thought it a bit strange, but I was curious nonetheless. I bent down next to her and poked her face, letting out a laugh back to her as she giggled at me.

"What are you drawing, Munchkin?" I asked.

"It's a bear, but he likes to be fancy!" she replied eagerly. "I want him to sing, too."

"Well, just give him a microphone," I said, picking up a pencil and drawing a mic in his hand. "There, he can sing all he wants now."

"Yeah, but now there's no one to play with him... I have to make friends."

I had a hard smile on. Only Lila could be such a

precious creature. I was the luckiest father alive to have the world's sweetest daughter.

"Think you can do that tomorrow? It's a little past your bedtime."

"Umm, do I get extra time tomorrow?" she asked, smiling.

"Of course, only if you help me put groceries away."

"Okay."

She put the pencil back on my wooden coffee table and got up, running to her room. As she got ready for bed, I too got up and put her canvas on top of the bookshelf, next to my wife's urn.

I waited a few minutes before walking into my daughter's room to tuck her in, as I knew she always took a long time to get ready for bed. As I waited, I checked the glass display case where I held the Hellstitcher's weapon from when Tony was killed. The tool of destruction was still sitting in place, exactly how I left it. The sword of necro-plated bones still gave a chilling sensation to my spine every time I looked at it. It was the object of fear. There were whispers of forgotten souls that seeped out from the millions of mouths it boasted. I kept the display case in my bedroom at all times so as to not scare Lila for the rest of her days living as a child.

I put the black cloth back over the case and exited my room. Before I came into Lila's room, I shut all the curtains in the house to buy her some more time. By the time I was done with all of this, Lila was finally ready to go to sleep.

"Hey, Lila," I said softly, opening her door.

"Hi, Daddy," she said back. She was already

lying in her bed under her midnight sky covers.

I bent down and swiftly pulled the covers over her head, immediately following it up with tickling her sides. Her laughter came out instantly, while she squirmed around on her sheets, trying to free herself.

I let go and let her recover from my onslaught of fatherly love. She fixed her blankets and smiled while avoiding eye contact with me, clearly trying not to burst out laughing again. I helped her out and let her rest at ease. Just like that, she was all ready to go to bed again.

"You gonna go to sleep anytime soon?" I asked.

"Yeah..." she slowly said, moving her long brown hair out of her eyes.

"Good, good," I said. "Hey, you're becoming quite the talented artist. You're reminding me of someone I used to know."

"Who?" she asked back.

"Ohhh, no one, just your mother. She was just impeccable at drawing whatever she imagined."

"Oh, I wish Mommy could see my drawings. Why did she leave?" she asked, her smile fading.

"Ah, Munchkin, you already know my answer..." I said, sadly dropping my eyes. "We'll see her again, believe me. With time, Mommy will stay with us forever."

"Okay."

A long pause interrupted us, giving our thoughts room to grow. Lila still was looking down, surely wondering where her mother was. I had to tell her eventually, but it's not the right time. Even though I hadn't told her yet, I had a feeling she already knew. Lila was a smart girl; it wouldn't surprise me a single bit.

"Hey," I started. "Good night, Munchkin. I love you, so much."

"Good night, Daddy," she said, a smile returning to her face. "I love you, too. Are you gonna say it?"

"Of course," I said, letting out a chuckle. I softly placed her hand in my own and set it onto my chest. I took a deep breath and spoke again. "Hold on to my heart, Lila."

She smiled and leaned in for a hug, squeezing me as hard as her arms could, before speaking back to me.

"I'm holding on."

Chapter Three

Kudos to me for a job well done; Sunders was no match. Like everyone else, he too was weak and helpless against the force of a Hellstitcher. How could I blame him? He's only human; he wasn't meant to stand up to such a force. Anyone who would take such an action would be foolish; no power on Earth could even harm me.

As I came back through my bloodportal, I smiled, thinking of Sunders' fate. If I was taking my best educated guess, I'd say his soul ended up here, in Hell. Perhaps if I visited the Library of the Damned, I could find him and continue to torment him beyond death. All I'd have to do was avoid Satan and his belligerence for a few hours.

I looked up to see Satan was already speaking to a demon, distracted enough to let me pass by. I took off, quietly striding toward the stone bridge that led to the main ground of Hell. I quickly looked behind me to see he was still preoccupied with the demon. Only a few seconds more would give me the distance I needed to be out of sight.

Only a few more steps...just a few more... I was

so close. Once I was out of range, I'd be home free. Sunders was about to get a whole variety of my methods, with a repentless force.

All of a sudden, I crashed into something and stumbled backward. It was Tenebris, grumpy as always. He, too, stumbled and almost fell over.

"Hey, what's the big idea, Decipere?" he shouted. "I thought you of all people would look where you're headed. You know, if you've got some place to be, you need a clear path. One without another Hellstitcher in the way."

"Would you do me a favor and sew your mouth shut?" I talked back. "If all you've got to say is just going to be useless, you may as well not talk."

Tenebris' expression stayed the exact same. It was like he had trouble reacting to others' words, like he wasn't even listening.

"Well, here's something useful for you to hear," he started. "I know how to get the jump on you, Decipere. I can catch you off guard, and if you don't believe me, maybe we can settle it in the coliseum."

"No," I said, shaking my head. I already had plans. There's no way I'd let a degenerate take them away.

"What? What do you mean, 'no'?" he said with a hint of complaint in his voice. "I said I can catch you off guard! Bah! Whatever, after knowing what I just learned, I'd beat you to a crippled mess in less than thirty seconds anyway. You're not worth my time!"

"If you're really surprised that I said 'no,' then maybe *I'm* the one who can catch *you* off guard," I said with a smirk. "It's to be expected, though. You're just naturally...less gifted, let's say."

"Watch it," he growled back. "You wouldn't last a second against me. You may win most of our battles, but not this time. This time, it will be you who begs for mercy."

Wrong, I won *all* of our battles. This troglodyte continued to exasperate my patience, but I couldn't do anything about it unless I agreed to fight him.

I stood and glared at Tenebris for a brief moment, then looked back at Satan sitting on his throne. He continued to talk to demons, but this time, a whole squad of five occupied his attention. Maybe...the library could wait, for now. Maybe I could use a good fight; I hadn't floored Tenebris in quite some time. His cockiness had inflated again, and it's time to cut it back down to size.

"Heh. I suppose you could use another ass-kicking," I said, looking back to him. "I've got no plans. I'll be at the coliseum waiting while you gather the others."

Tenebris gave one last look of annoyance before walking away. He broke out running, heading toward the Food Sanctuary. I, too, started along my way, destination coliseum. Satan was much easier to evade than I first assumed, but it didn't mean he couldn't call me from across Hell. Luckily for me, he hadn't noticed my arrival yet.

It took a good ten minutes to reach the coliseum. Demons were already in the stands, cheering on an ongoing fight. I stepped into the steely stairwell and looked through a window to see three demons duking it out, free-for-all style. One was clearly injured and was limping to dodge attacks.

I came up the rest of the stairwell, into the stands. A group of demons was eyeing me as I walked through, as though I was an outsider barging into their territory. I walked all the way around the arena to the announcer's seat. Memories of this coliseum flooded my mind. So many candidates for the Hellstitchers once fought here, and they were slain by my hand. I remembered every one of them. Sitting at the announcer's seat was another demon, wearing the signature brown cloak and hood that announcers always had to wear. She didn't see me at first, but I stood and waited to see how long it would take her to notice my presence.

Only a few seconds later, she tilted her fiery head my way and gasped as she realized I was waiting. She yelled and fell out of the seat, taking off running. I chuckled and stood on the seat, facing the crowd.

"Gladiators!" I yelled, with the entire coliseum now turned to me. I held a smug look on my face, my arms raised. "Be grateful you have another day to live. I will now be taking over the arena. Those who wish to watch may stay, but for the ones who don't...well, you *also* have to stay. Don't care if you enjoy the show or not. Anyway, allow me to announce the two contenders. Our challengers are...me, Decipere the

Monger, and Tenebris the Incompetent."

The wave of demons let out ear-bleeding laughs and screams. A few threw rocks into the air to cheer me on. The primitive beasts were difficult to like... I wished they were at least a bit smart in some way. Once I took over Hell, they would all bend to me whether they liked it or not, and I would train them to be the best warriors Hell had ever laid eyes on.

I reveled in their praise and raised my arms up, nodding and looking all over the stands. My smile was quickly erased when Tenebris finally arrived, along with the other Hellstitchers. Gomorrah was the last in line and was hunched over, eyes twitching at the crowd. That deranged abomination needed to be put out of his misery, even if I did lead him...

Gomorrah may be the worst Hellstitcher out of all of us. His insanity led him to do risky moves on the job; I was constantly wondering why he hadn't been reverted into a normal demon or straight-up killed. I remembered the moment that took his sanity away from him. Back in the gladiatorial days, he had a partner in combat that he rose to the top with named Sodom. It was the contest that chose the Hellstitchers that killed him off. Their opponents were smart and were able to lead Gomorrah's own cudgel into Sodom's brain. After barely surviving that battle, Gomorrah had a massive head injury and a dead partner that he himself accidentally killed. He only spiraled down from there.

Atrocify gave me a bored look as I stood over the

sandy battlefield. He was certainly not impressed that me and Tenebris were going at it again. I didn't care, though. He can go back to his meal once the fight was over and I was standing over Tenebris' struggling body once again. He turned to Immolatus and started talking, but I couldn't read their lips.

The Hellstitchers rose to the stands and took front row seats to the show.

"A-ha! I guess you are all done with your contracts, didn't expect all of us to be here," I boomed, letting everyone hear my voice. "But that's just better! I want *everyone* to be reminded of just how much better I am than this...eh, invertebrate."

From across the stage, Tenebris approached with an enraged expression. He revealed two of his prized battle axes from behind his back and threw his arms out to the side, as if to say, "Here I am." Alas, that beast would be no match for me; I had conquered him many times before, and I would do it again today. My resentment for him did not reach the amount I had for the Devil, but it's oh so close. His weakness disgusted me...and his constant attempts to get the better of me were revolting.

Demons of red and black filled the stands and cried out for bloodshed. The coliseum was now full enough to the point where there were demons flying in the air just to get a view. The coliseum was so close to fitting the entire legion in. Once I seized Hell, I'd order to have it rebuilt into a bigger stadium.

I leaped down from the announcer's seat and

onto the grainy floor of the battleground. Fifty feet away from me was my opponent: Tenebris. With steely axes in hand, he took a defensive stance. His red eyes shined into mine, and his curved horns pierced my mind. I, too, took ahold of my weapon. From the back strap of my satchel lay my morningstar, the Jugulator. Its bronze casting had ceased the lives of many, but still, it hungered for more.

"I am ready, Decipere!" Tenebris yelled. "You know, you don't have to be an asshole to me around *everyone.*"

"What was that?" I yelled back, a hand to my ear. "I couldn't hear you. I'm partially brainless."

More laughter erupted from the crowd, along with Immolatus booing my snarky remark. He could take all the offense he wanted, but I cared not about it.

Tenebris let out a yell and switched from a defensive stance to a charge, rapidly heading toward my location. I waited for him to get too close before I made a move. His yelling grew louder and louder as he closed in, and yet I stood still.

Suddenly, the time was now. As Tenebris lunged at me, I swiftly dropped to the floor and kicked my feet up, sending my enemy into the air. With a loud thud, he smacked the ground a second later. As he fell to the floor, I rose and slowly walked to him.

He recovered just as I arrived, and he dodged a kick aimed for his face. I followed it up with a swing of my morningstar, barely scratching his moving body.

He rushed me down in my opening and slammed me to the floor. I let out a groan, along with a fierce growl. The nerve of this demon was going to lead to his death!

Being only inches away from his face, I stunned him with a headbutt, immediately giving me my opportunity to escape. I let out a flurry of blows that continued to discombobulate Tenebris and finished it off with a powerful backhand that knocked him to the ground once again. The cheers from the legion continued to rage on, and their unified battle cry was louder than a nuclear detonation.

My breathing was beginning to feel heavy, as if I was out of shape. Sure, I hadn't battled in some time, but I was still the Monger! Residing in me was a power and stamina that rivaled no other! Even if Tenebris *did* manage to get the jump on me, he had little chance of claiming victory.

"Who are you, little man?!" I yelled, mocking him. "This isn't a dance party. This is a fight! You knew that, right?"

Nothing but another yell came from Tenebris. He bolted toward me again, but I easily countered it with a quick side-step punch to the ribs. He growled and slid away from me, immediately chucking one of his axes at my chest. With less than a second to react, I blocked the axe with my arm, taking the full blade into my stony skin.

I let out a cry of pain and ripped the axe out. With a mighty thrust, I tossed it into the crowd, landing it into the skull of a demon cheering the fight on. Blood spewed from both my victim and my forearm, forcing out even more of my anger. I leaped toward Tenebris and swung my Jugulator at him, to no avail. He was swift for sure, but I was bound to land a shot eventually.

More yells came out as I let go of my weapon mid-swing, letting it fly at my target. Tenebris attempted a risky block with his axe, but I charged him as he was distracted, letting me gain advantage of the scene. I lifted him high into the sky and forcefully threw him into the ground, an earth-shattering stomp crushing his left hand. Cries of pain left him as he writhed on the floor. He was fully disarmed now, but so was I. Now, the battle was only about our fists and how we used them. Fortunately for me, I had just ravaged one of his hands. The battle was tipped toward me, as it always would be.

"Wait, all right!" Tenebris groaned. "You can have this round. I don't want to fight anymore!"

I stood in awe. I was utterly shocked at this forfeit; there was no match in history between us where a surrender took place. What could have come over Tenebris? How could he possibly give up so early on? Perhaps he was finally realizing his true worth, being the worst demon of all. I turned a perplexed look toward the other Hellstitchers, with Atrocify also giving one back. He shrugged his shoulders and looked at the others. While Immolatus was also trying to figure out what was going on, Gomorrah was only clawing at his own hands, clearly not paying any sort of attention. I rolled my eyes and looked back to Tenebris.

The cheering of the crowd was now turning into outrage, their cries of glory now transforming into screams of agony. Demons started throwing rocks again, none with any notable accuracy.

"You can't quit this early!" I said angrily. "We've only just begun, and you already decided to give up?! Why did you even—" I stopped myself for a moment, remembering exactly why he wanted to fight in the first place. He wanted to catch me off guard, but so far that hadn't happened yet. Either that, or I already ruined his plans. But...I couldn't be absolutely certain just yet... Perhaps he was attempting a false surrender. That was the only option I could see, and if that's what he's trying to pull, he's doing a lacking job of it. He may have surprised me for a second, but I could see through his act like a sheet of glass.

"Decipere..." he started, while getting to his feet. "I know I wanted this battle, but being beaten so quickly just doesn't feel right. It never has. Every time you beat me, I can't help but feel worthless. It's not even close, and it makes me wonder why I'm a Hellstitcher in the first place."

He trudged in front of me, now getting close. I had to stay alert. If he pulled anything, I needed to catch it before it gave him an advantage. Dirty play was *my* thing, and my thing only. A glare from my end froze him in place, directly in front of me. My eyes watched every bit of his body like a hawk.

"You can take this win, Decipere. I'm—" He suddenly cut himself off and launched a surprise fake-out. My reflexes were like a bolt of lightning. They flowed through his attack and struck back, landing a flat-palm smack into his nostrils. That filthy whelp would never get away with dirty tactics! Not in my fight!

I approached Tenebris, who was still clutching his face after the devastating blow. The cheers from the stadium skyrocketed, and I felt even more invigorated than before. Pissed and full of vengeance, I grappled onto his arms with my own and pulled them down to the ground. My knee went the other way, and its path was met with the chin of my victim. Tenebris stumbled over and turned away as he finally ejected the stalagmites from his body. Him using his powers first was always a sign of weakness; it meant he'd already lost and was desperate to find a way out.

"You think you can get away with such a dirty move?!" I screamed at him. "You ought to be punished! You cannot catch *me* off guard with those sorts of tricks! They belong to me!"

"At least I tried something new!" he screamed back, bleeding heavily from every spot on his face. "You deserve to be just as bad as me, if not worse! It's not fair you were made stronger than everyone else!"

"A-ha, but I'm not just stronger than everyone, Tenebris," I said, quickly walking to him. "I'm also smarter!"

I dodged a weak punch and took ahold of one of his spikes, ramming him into my chest and staggering him again. He was beginning to fall apart, knowing his big plan had just been razed.

"And I'm faster, too!" I yelled again, speeding up my movement. I flung a kick to his knee and tripped him after pulling him back toward me. He dropped to the sand once again and slowly lifted his head off the ground. His one good hand started to grip the floor beneath him, and he tried to lift himself up.

"What do you have over me, Tenebris?!" I said, stomping him back to the ground, destroying one of his rocky spikes. "You are a pathetic excuse for a Hellstitcher! You deserve to feel worthless, and you deserve to lose every fight! The only thing you're good at is reminding me of how poor a warrior you are."

"Gah! Shut up and get off me!" Tenebris yelled back. "You already won!"

"Yes, and you already lost again! This has been a waste of my time. You should be ashamed... Poor Tenebris, so weak and flimsy, you can't win a battle to save anyone's life."

"I said get off! I'm sick of hearing you boast and boast and boast! Why can't you just let me go without making a fool out of me?!"

I let out a wicked laugh and pointed. I looked around the cheering coliseum and continued laughing. This victory sure wasn't difficult, but it felt good nonetheless! There's nothing quite like putting Tenebris in his place. I looked to the other Hellstitchers to see that Immolatus had left already, and Gomorrah was still unable to pay attention.

Atrocify was watching but was giving me the sarcastic eyebrow.

"I'll tell you why!" I said, looking back at the cretin beneath me. "It's because you *are* a fool! You are nothing but a volatile loser, and losers don't even have names. You're only a nobody, and that's why I make a fool out of you."

A struggling groan came from Tenebris, as he suddenly rolled over and jumped to his feet, backing away from me. I gave him a smirk with my eyebrows furrowed. In return, he only glared, his teeth revealing his true anger. He continued to back away and soon turned to the doorway that led outside of the arena. It was blocked by the metal gate, but it was no match for him. He lifted it with ease and stormed out of the coliseum.

I raised a bleeding arm to the sky and celebrated my easy victory. The legion was still cheering me on, and I enjoyed every second of it. The more praise that came my way, the quicker my pride grew. Though Tenebris threw a curveball my way, I was still able to seize control and steal the win just as easily as every other time. Today's battle was short and sweet for a change, but I still wanted more action. One weak Hellstitcher wasn't enough.

"Anyone else want a beat down by the Monger?" I announced. "I don't know if that was a good enough fight for all of you!"

The audience roared, and a handful of demons flew out of the stands onto the bloody battlescape. All were equipped with their tridents and lances and murmuring their wicked thoughts. They quickly formed a circle around me, cutting me off from retrieving my weapon. I side-eyed the ones quietly approaching me, watching their slow and methodical movements carefully.

I decided to strike first and tip them off balance immediately. I raised my arms to my sides and shot out bursts of lava, melting the skin off the demons on the side. Their howls quickly faded with the cries of the other contenders. I dropped to the ground and threw myself backward, knocking a demon behind me to the ground, subsequently getting crushed by my enormous gray body. The other demons charged and began their assault as I was still on the ground.

Within moments of getting my chest penetrated, I ripped out the corpse from under my torso and shielded myself from the spear-tips of a trident. One raging kick from my end was able to send the attacker into the air, giving me a small opening to get on my feet. Two more demons charged, only to get swindled by my reaction time, grabbing their weapons mid-strike and stealing them away. A smack from the lance knocked one of the demons into the other, and I followed it up with jabbing both with the trident, earning myself a double kill. Throwing it away, I stormed through the rest of the crowd, only being harmed by my own gaining fatigue.

I laughed harder the more I killed! Nothing was getting past my wretched offense, and I didn't even need my morningstar to prove it. One by one, my challengers fell. Amongst the dying bodies, blood ran everywhere. Screams and cries rushed forth, and screams of pain and agony ripped the air like a butcher knife.

And then, it was done. My arms were blood-soaked, and my throat was dry. This was a better fight than what Tenebris gave me. Maybe it's because it was easier, or maybe it's because it lasted a little longer. I cared not about the difficulty of the fight; I always would come out on top. Applause stained the sky and hydrated my strength. It was a worthy series of battles, regardless of who I fought. My valiant efforts continued to gain the support from the watchful crowd. I let out a scream and yelled along with the audience. Once again, I bathed in the applause, knowing my victory was deserved.

"Decipere!" a loud voice boomed. The crowd went silent, as they knew who approached. The Devil loomed over the coliseum, rearing his lava-dripping face. Instantly, I dropped to my knees and bowed down to Lucifer.

"What do you need of me, sire?" I spoke, clearly agitated at his intervention.

"What I *need* from you, Decipere, is your trustworthiness!" he yelled. "You cannot just sneak past me when I am speaking to others. Your contract has finished, but I had another one waiting for you!"

Clearly, I *could* just sneak past him, as demonstrated half an hour ago. However, this new contract surprised me, as it was extremely quick. The other Hellstitchers managed to finish theirs before I did, but Satan opted to give another one to me anyway. How curious...

"How quick that was, Satan," I said. "Why weren't any of the other Hellstitchers assigned to this? I was already working on mine."

"It's a punishment, you insolent bastard," Satan growled. "Your attitude toward me needs correction, and seeing as you snuck off and started messing around, I believe it's even more deserving. Oh, and I'm not refilling your Sulfric Growlers yet. You'll live without them."

"I understand," I said. I clenched my teeth in frustration, irritated at my master. Soon...he would be the one to be punished, by my hand. It's just a matter of time before I found out how.

"Come to the throne. I'll have your contractor's name up here," he said calmly before turning away and walking back to his seat.

I rose to my feet and looked to Atrocify, still sitting in the stands. I beckoned him with my hand, walking his way. He too rose and dropped to the arena sands. We met in the middle of the coliseum, with most of the demons quietly leaving the stands.

"Think you can do me a favor, slip me a couple Sulfric Growlers?" I asked with a slightly desperate tone. "You know I always repay you."

"Decipere..." Atrocify said, raising a hand to his head. "You can't keep doing this; once Satan finds out, you'll be in even more trouble. I want to help, but this might be the last time."

"That's all right," I said. "I'm working on using less and less. I'm getting better at it. Soon you'll be the one repaying *me*." This very obviously wasn't true, but I was not about to work on another contract without at least one.

"Yeah, is that so?" Atrocify laughed. He reached in his satchel and took out two Sulfric Growlers, dropping them in my hand. "We'll see about that."

"Don't worry about it for a second," I told him, putting the capsules in my own satchel. I was going to put these to very good use, but I'd probably have to be sparing.

Atrocify began walking out of the coliseum, and I strode next to him. At the path that led to the throne, I gave him a salute and continued to walk my own way. He returned my salute with one of his own, with a very bored expression. I walked and walked and walked, and once enough time passed, I arrived at my destination: the throne.

Chapter Four

UNWISE

Satan was waiting for me, scroll in hand. He was already shrunken down to a miniature size, still towering over me. His expression told of satisfaction. Punishment on me was clearly his form of enjoyment, but it wouldn't be that way forever.

I gave him a glare and held out my hand. My glare was returned with a despicable smile and the scroll of my new contractor. I held it up to my face and scowled at the name. It was a Whitewinter. Rodney Whitewinter. I'd served a Whitewinter before, from the exact same place. It'd been several years since I'd done this; perhaps this was the son, or even a grandson. It had been so long.

"Another Whitewinter?" I asked sarcastically.

"Yes, I knew you'd enjoy seeing your friends again," the Devil said with a menacing grin. "I'm sure you'll have the same amount of fun as you did last time."

Satan's cocky attitude drove me insane. How it would please me to no end to rip the molten red skin right off his face...

When I first did a contract for a Whitewinter, I went through an unreasonable amount of trouble to get my kill. It took me four days to complete it...which was saying a lot, considering my history. It was egregious and unnecessary; I hated every minute of it. Perhaps this time it would be different. It better be different.

I gave an audible growl of frustration and stormed to my bloodportal. My destination was Mississippi, the Magnolia State. For as beautiful as it could be there, its residents could be quite the opposite. As I continued dwelling on the state, I arrived at my portal. As it stood in front of me, I ripped it open with a vicious thrust and stepped in.

***

The dank and humid air barraged me when I exited my portal. I felt a scent of smoke entering my nostrils, reminding me of my last encounter with a Whitewinter. The room I was in was the exact same as so long ago. An ugly gray carpeting, a single window directly opposite from my person, and even the same wooden wallpaper greeted me for the second time. This time, though...there was a massive, boarded-up hole on one of the walls. It wasn't too unfamiliar, however, as I was the one who created the behemoth of a hole.

I looked down to the floor, and in front of the ritual's layout sat three very young men. Teenagers, I had to assume. That's just wonderful. If a group of teenagers was summoning a Hellstitcher, they weren't doing it for business: they were doing a dare.

One of the teenagers, the middle one, had gaping wide eyes focused on mine. His mouth was slowly opening as wide as his eyes, and he leaned back ever so slightly. This was Rodney Whitewinter, no doubt about it.

The other two boys held no change of expression, as they were not the ones who summoned me. Only Rodney could see me, but that could change...

"Well, I knew this was all a bunch of bullshit," the teen on the left said.

"You're the one who wanted to do it," the other one said. "Hey, Rod, you all right?"

Rodney didn't say anything but just raised a frightened finger and pointed at me.

"What the hell is he pointing at?" the first teen asked, furrowing his eyebrows.

"I dunno, maybe the Hellstitcher is really here," the second one replied.

I gave a sinister smile to Rodney and lifted my yellow hand up to wave.

"Hello, Rodney," I said grimly.

He let out a gasp and slowly backed away on the floor. His second friend put his arm on Rodney's shoulder to reassure his assumed safety, but Rodney didn't calm down whatsoever.

"Monroe, it's here..." Rodney said, tears beginning to fall.

"Rod, it can't be here. Me and Brad don't see anything," Monroe said calmly, trying to settle Rodney down.

"Yeah, if it was here, then we'd be able to see it!" Brad yelled. "You can't pretend to be a baby to fool me."

"Your friends can't see me, Rodney," I began. "Unless I decide to...*influence* them. You're the one who laid the snake down. Therefore you're the one who gives me my contract."

I couldn't believe I had to explain these things to this kid... He should never have summoned me, unless he had a real plan to have someone killed.

"I-I...I don't want you to kill anyone," Rodney said with a pale expression. "We just wanted to see if you were real..."

"Rod, there's nothing there," Monroe blurted.

"Yeah...there's nothing here," I said, smiling wider.

"This is a waste of time. Let's just put this shit away," Brad said with a frustrated tone.

"No, guys, it's *actually* here," Rod argued, tears still streaming.

"Here, allow me to help," I said, now approaching Monroe.

"No! Wait! What are you going to do?!" Rodney yelled.

"Rod, what are you *talking* about?" Monroe said, now gaining a frightened voice.

Suddenly, Monroe's face transitioned from a state of fear into a form of disgust, smelling the sulfuric stench of my Sulfric Growler. I only had one left, but I'd use that for my next contract. By then, Satan would surely grant me more.

The expressions of Monroe quickly morphed again, locking eyes with my own. He let out a yelp and scooted back, still focused on my demonic presence. His long brunette hair fell into his face and was quickly pulled back again. His fear, like Rodney's, was under my control. This was too much fun...

"I—I— Wha?!" he yelled with a stutter.

"You see it?!" Rodney yelled back, still pointing a finger.

"Yes, I see it!" Monroe began. "How come I didn't see it before?! What are you?"

"Hahaha! You fools!" I laughed. "You have no idea of what you just unleashed!"

"What the hell are you two crying about?" Brad said. "There's still nothing there! You assholes are trying to pull some sort of sick joke on me, aren't you?"

"Brad, no!" Monroe said, standing up. "The Hellstitcher is here, it really is! It's laughing at us."

Rodney nodded and threw his head to the floor, avoiding the grotesque sight that stood before him.

"Yeah? Well, how come *I* can't see it, huh?" Brad argued back. "We did the ritual, and nothing happened. You two are just trying to get back at me for making you do this!"

Monroe and Rodney were clearly being oppressed here. I got it now... But if they didn't have a contract for me, then Whitewinter would have to die. Unfortunate that it had come to this, but it didn't bother me in the slightest. I just kept on laughing.

"Brad...listen to us!" Rodney cried. "The thing is here! I don't know why you can't see it!"

"You shut your mouth, Whitewinter!" Brad yelled back, also standing up. "The Hellstitchers aren't real, anyway! It's all a bunch of myths and lies that your crazy grandfather told you. Hell, I bet the Devil isn't even real!"

My laughter stopped and was replaced by a scowl followed by a death stare into Brad's brown eyes. I was enjoying myself, but now my rage had taken over. This boy had nerve to forsake me! How dare he?

"What did he just say?!" I roared, fire blazing from the depths of my pupils.

"You made him angry, Brad..." Monroe said in a

whisper. "I think we all just need to calm dow—"

"No, no, no, I don't think you get it," Brad interrupted. He paused to slick back his silky blond hair. "I can see through your dumbass plan! You think that just because 'oh, I'm such an awful friend' you have the right to put on a freak show and expect me to believe it! The Hellstitchers aren't real!"

"You'd better get your pal to shut up or I'll make sure he ends up as a pile of rat food when I'm done with him!" I yelled in an act of resentment. I was in flames, ready to tear this boy limb from limb. I wanted to squeeze the organs out of his body...slowly.

"If you don't believe they're real, then why'd you make us do this in the first place?!" Monroe yelled back at him. He was beginning to pale as much as Rodney was, fearing the wrath my muscles could bring upon.

"Oh, please," Brad stated with a calmer tone. "Weren't you listening at all yesterday? You guys are supposed to prove you aren't a couple of pussies, but congratulations, you've actually just instead lost the friend in me."

"The Hellstitcher is still here, guys," Rodney muttered.

Even though I heard him, I barely even paid attention to what was said. I was still fixated on the soon-to-be rotting corpse. His big body...it was irresistible to my destruction. The silver-and-gold prized watch on his wrist especially demanded my violent nature; this boy would be punished!

"What did I just say, Whitewinter?" Brad yelled again. "It isn't real. It's. A. Myth. A myth! Anyone who believes in that stuff belongs in an insane asylum!"

"Argh! You, boy, are getting it!" I bellowed, approaching Brad.

"Wait, Hellstitcher, what are you gonna do?!" Monroe begged.

"I will show him what to believe in," I said. A stern and vengeful voice took over as I reached the boy.

"Wait, no!" a yell came out, a little too late.

A shower of blood suddenly erupted from Brad's shoulder, and with it, his arm was completely torn off. Screams of agony and suffering echoed throughout the state, not just from my victim, but also from the two bystanders witnessing their peer's amputation. Bloodstains littered the wallpaper and the carpeting. A mess had been made by my hands once again, and it made me feel so alive! I felt as though I had to do more, more desecration of this child's worthless body! His ignorance would not be tolerated by the likes of the Monger!

I threw the screaming bully to the floor and picked him up again by the torso and the legs. The limbs were constantly flailing about, but I kept my arms steady. My stony body took a position of power, and with a loud and jarring roar, I pulled with all my might and tore his entire person apart!

All sorts of organs and meats dropped from the mounting chaos. Blood was a given, but the extra contents that spilled over the ugly carpet was too good of a reward. The satisfying sound of this human's body getting ripped apart bedazzled my senses; I felt as if I had already conquered life itself. The screaming that burst out of this boy came to a halt, and replacing it were his tissues, organs, and blood. Maybe it *was* against the rules to kill a human, but not if it's isolated from a contract. I may be stretching the rule like taffy, but I wouldn't be demoted for it. I shouldn't.

The screaming from the other two suddenly ended, and all that came from them was an expression of shock and awe. Carefully backing away, they continued to stare directly at the massacre I had created, surely hoping they wouldn't be next.

"Time for your contract, Whitewinter," I said in a deep voice, breathing heavily from the murder I'd just committed.

Rodney didn't hesitate to make his next move; he quickly snatched Monroe by the arm and booked it out of his room. The screaming revved up again as they made their way out of my presence.

"Hey! You can't—" I started. It was too late; only a couple seconds later, I heard the opening of the front door, followed by a starting engine. They were about to get away.

If I couldn't catch them in time, I'd be demoted into the ranks of the legion of demons. I had only a week to do this... I could wait for their return, but perhaps it'd be best to hunt them down. They would have to give me a contract once I reached them, or else they would have to perish. I had nothing against punishing those who attempted to back out.

I let out a grunt of frustration and then a chuckle. I stepped up to the room opposite to the boarded-up wall and set myself up to a readying stance. A deep breath exhaled from my mouth, and I gazed upon the poorly constructed "fixed" wall. With ninja speed, my legs bolted me forward. Head tucked and forearms jutted out, my body smashed through the walls once again.

I landed on my feet, surrounded by walls of tall grass. The loud driving of a speeding car was still being picked up by my amplified sense of hearing, letting me know exactly where to go. As I walked out of the grass, I looked back at the massive hole gaping from the house wall. I still smelled the stench of leaking blood. Everywhere I went...it seemed all I could do was cause damage. That truth had already been clear to me, but it felt like it didn't have to be that way. As much as I loved seeing things fall apart by my hand, it's a sad way of life. I knew this but still accepted my reality. Why try to change yourself when you could not? I'd grown to enjoy it more, and that's the only way I could live. It's the only way I wanted to live.

Turning my attention back toward the issue at hand, I leaped out of the tall grass, and with a loud thud, I ended up on the road. Under the night sky, I began a quick run directed at the retreating vehicle, carefully dodging innocent cars along the way. As fast as I was running, the teenagers' car was beginning to fade away. This was about to end up just like my first contract with a Whitewinter, but I was not going to let that happen.

I picked up the pace into a sprint. My muscular and athletic body dominated the road; I was riding on the wind. The fading runaway car was coming back into the picture, and I could only get closer. As soon as I reached that boy, I was going to turn that car of his into little bits of scrap metal.

Seconds passed by, and with that, my eyes eventually laid eyes on my target. It was a rusty and red Chevy Malibu, clearly from before its owner's time. It was speeding away passing the other occupants of the road, endangering everyone on it. If the police got to them first, my contract may have to wait even longer.

With one final grunt, I let out a burst of energy and thrusted toward the car. I quickly jabbed at one of the back tires and blew it to pieces. The Malibu immediately swerved to the other side of the road and struck a roll. I finally slowed myself to a stop and gasped for breath while watching the car continue to crash.

Several cars kept driving by when it slowed to a stop. The two boys quickly got out and fell to the ground. I started walking their way, still breathing heavily but feeling accomplished. Rodney and Monroe sat down against the side of the totaled car, speaking to each other. I couldn't tell what they were saying, but I needed their attention.

"You boys have caused me more trouble than I ever needed!" I yelled, still striding toward them. I haunted them as I approached with a cold stare of death. "Don't think you can escape me again. I've got senses beyond your imaginations, and I *will* hunt you down again if I need to."

"What do you want from us?!" Rodney yelled in a desperate voice.

"I want my contract!" I roared back. "I have a job to do, and you're making it difficult! Just give me the name of someone I can kill!"

Rodney stood up and backed away, still locked on to my person. The cars were still passing by, no one even giving a slight care about bothering the injured drivers. In this day and age, that was the norm. Rodney had no one to rescue him from my demands.

"I don't want anyone to die!" he complained. "We didn't know you actually existed... Brad made us do it. He dared us to prove we weren't a couple of cowards. I told him about the story of the Hellstitchers...and you can just guess the rest of what happened."

"You are a foolish child," I scolded. "If it were up to me, all three of you would be shredded by my fingertips. You are unwise and in need of correction. I believe I have already done that." I paused to bend over and speak to him up close. "Now, Whitewinter, I need a contract."

"We don't have one for you!" Monroe interrupted. "We aren't gonna let anyone die, so you can get lost, Hellstitcher."

"You don't understand, hippie," I growled. "I am forced by my code. If you refuse to give me a contract, I will be required to kill you. I will have to kill Rodney, in particular."

"What?! Why?" Rodney yelled. "Can't you just reject the contract?"

"Why him?" Monroe butted in again. "Why would you have to kill him instead of both of us or just me? That's not fair."

"Unfortunately for everyone, life isn't fair." I spoke calmly. "Even for me, it isn't fair. I'm bound by Satan's rules, and if I don't follow them, I'll have to die. Any way you look at it, someone has to die. Right now, it can be me, Rodney, or any human he chooses. If he doesn't want to choose, then I'll have to kill him. The only silver lining is that you won't have to sell your soul if you choose not to give a contract, but maybe you were already going to Hell anyway."

I didn't tell them that if I failed to kill the target, I would instead be demoted. They would be able to keep their soul if that happened, and I suspected they'd try to give me a near-impossible target if they knew that. Chances were they didn't have a target I couldn't kill, but I wouldn't take that chance. I *would* kill whoever I needed to kill. That option was usually kept secret from those who changed their minds, which wasn't many, but they did pop up.

"So...if I want to live, I'll have to sell my soul and pick someone to die?" Rodney said quietly.

"That's what I said," I said in a sarcastic tone. "It angers me to no end having to explain all of this to you. Usually contractors have at least a little bit of understanding of what they're doing when they're summoning a Hellstitcher."

"Yeah, but we're kids! Do your rules say anything about exceptions for kids?" Monroe blurted.

"What do you think?" I said, slightly irritated. "We only have one purpose, and we don't discriminate. If you lay the snake down during the ritual, you will have to give the contract, no matter who you are."

A long moment of silence fell, with both teenagers deep in thought. I closed my eyes, awaiting a response.

The seconds passed by slowly. As time went on, I only grew more and more impatient. This whole contract was a waste of time.

"I... Okay... I understand," Rodney said, breaking the silence. "Monroe...I-I don't want to do this. I think we need to choose someone."

"Yeah," Monroe grunted, staring at the grass

below him.

"Who can we choose, though? It's awful of us to do this..."

"Then we choose someone who's *also* awful!" Monroe yelled with his hands over his head.

"Uh, okay..." Rodney said, offended by Monroe's outburst. "I, uh...Hellstitcher, I want you to kill Reese Wurthers. He's a bully at our high school. Probably the worst out of all of them."

"He's a crook, too," Monroe said. "He likes to steal things from the cafeteria. I've heard he's shoplifted a lot, as well."

I instantly picked up a new scent, this one belonging to my new target. Reese Wurthers was already close by... I was going to have to skip the day of stalking for this contract. I didn't want to spend any more time on Whitewinter.

"Go back to your house," I told Rodney. "The next time I see you will be when Wurthers is dead. Count on it. If I don't see you at your house within twenty-four hours, I will hunt you down again, and believe me, I will not *hesitate* to tear you apart like I did with Blondie."

Whitewinter made an audible gulp and sat back down on the grass. I turned back to the road, and a bloodportal appeared before my eyes. Just in time, a car began to slow and parked on the shoulder of the road. A tall woman exited the vehicle and called for the boys, but this was where I left them for now. I had another child to kill.

***

My bloodportal took me into a nearby city. Its foul stench filled my nostrils with agony. I gagged before realizing I was in a large open parking lot, only partly filled with cars. The midnight sun above me shined down on an outdoor food court a short distance away. Wurthers was there. Among the scents of litter and polluted air, I picked up Wurthers again and started on my way to the food court.

The busy roads occupied my hearing. All of the honking and revving gave me a sense of nostalgia. I'd always loved being in the cities. My favorite contract had me in a city called Tokyo. Its beauty was what made me enjoy them, that and all of the absurd things that could happen. That contract's victim was knocked out of a skyscraper and fell to the earth for an entire ten seconds before slamming into the ground. It was marvelous.

As I reached the food court, I noticed the sheer number of people there. Probably over sixty, I'd say. Picking Reese out of them shouldn't be a problem, however. He had to be here; my senses could not be wrong.

I looked around at all of the people. Chatter and crinkles of wrappers were now the only sounds I could hear. There were three noticeably big men in the crowd; one of them ought to be Wurthers. I'd been around long enough to know bullies. They were oftentimes the victims of my contracts, and most of them definitely deserved the punishment.

I walked up to the first, the closest, of the three options. I gave him a smirk and moved on. He wasn't giving off the scent at all. The second one was in line to get his meal, but I still got up close and personal with him. As long as no one saw me, I'd be perfectly fine. Such a thing was impossible, but the thought of it happening still lurked in the back of my mind.

This second man wasn't Wurthers, either; he gave off a wretched scent worse than the first. I had to move on, for this last one had to be my man.

"Reese!" I yelled, casually approaching the big teenager. "How've you been? I heard Tom and Marie broke up. Think you can get a second chance with her?"

The teenager kept about his business, completely oblivious to the storm about to come over him. I wished I could use another Sulfric Growler, but I still only had the one left.

"Hey, listen, don't tell anyone, but I think Tom was cheating on her, y'know?" I said with a laid-back attitude. Poking fun at my victims never got old. "He was always that player type. No girl could ever last with him for more than a month, which is a shame, because I think if he really tried, he could be an excellent boyfriend for them. For one of them, obviously. I mean I don't wanna be 'that guy,' but we both know he's never gonna *actually* try and do that."

I laughed at the bit I just played out. I never kept track of the little stories I made, but they're fun to lay on to victims, especially the ones I infused with a Sulfric Growler.

I once again got up close to the man and gave him a good whiff. The scent was slightly off... I was sure that this boy was who I was looking for. This one wasn't Wurthers, either!

I growled and looked back into the crowd. The scent was still here, but where was it coming from?! I would have to filter them out if I wanted to find Wurthers. The crowd was getting larger, too. I needed to find him very quickly before he escaped my grasp.

I was able to get close enough to the customers looking to be young enough to be a teenager. One by one, I gripped their scents and moved on. Wurthers was beginning to slip away, and I could feel it within my stone-like skin. The worry began to settle in my mind, and I wondered if I had already lost him. If he escaped, I might have to continue this contract for another day.

My movements became quicker. I was switching from person to person within a flash of light. As Wurthers continued to evade my wrath, I continued to press on the search. My person was a hunter, and I was getting closer...closer to my prey. He wasn't far away; I could tell I was about to meet him.

My nostrils were taking a beating, but I was so close! Almost there... Almost there... He's so close I could taste his flesh. He's right...

Here! I stepped back and gazed at the wonder upon me. A little boy, surely not taller than five foot five, was eating his wrap alone. His long hair was dyed silver and brushed to perfection. He almost looked as if he was about to cry. This couldn't be Reese Wurthers, could it?

I gave him another good, long whiff. This was him, all right, but why did he look like the complete opposite of a bully? There was no one he was talking to, and he looked to prefer it that way. If this boy really was the worst bully in Rodney's life, it'd mean my perception of them was purely skewed. It was black and white when I thought it to be a grayscale.

Lessons aside...I still needed to end this boy's life. Him not being at home made it that much more challenging to find things he cared about. I gazed at him, up and down, unable to find anything symbolizing value. As I eyeballed his gray hoodie, he kept on eating his wrap, almost finishing it off at this point.

I took a step back and observed. There had to be something I was missing... I couldn't just follow this boy everywhere until he went home. I'd done it with every other contract, but I wouldn't do it with this one. Whitewinter was bound to supply more trouble the longer I stayed.

Wait! A small glimmer shined from behind his hoodie's collar. It's a necklace! That could be what I was looking for. If I incinerated the necklace and he didn't die, I might just have to follow him home. There's nothing else of note he's showing...

I walked back up to the boy and lightly tapped on his shoulder, turning his attention away from the meal. With delicate and precise accuracy, I reached my hand out to grab the necklace string with my nails. Once I made contact, I was home free.

Suddenly, he turned his head back to the sandwich, forcing me to quickly retreat my hand away. I growled in a fit of frustration and lightly pushed forward on his back. He shot up from his seat and glared at the people behind him. One man in particular caught his glare and gave him a confused look, unaware of his aggressor's anger toward him.

"You think it's funny to mess with me?!" Wurthers cried out. "You think it's funny to pick on the little guys, huh?"

"What...the hell are you talking about?" the man asked, looking around the food court.

"Don't play stupid with me, shithead! I know what you're up to!" Wurthers blasted back, rapidly approaching the man. He got up to his face and stood on his toes to meet the man's eyes.

"Look, man, I di—" the man started before getting cut off.

"You didn't what?! Try and mess with me and act like you don't know what's going on?" Wurthers yelled while drawing in a crowd. I was still in the middle, prepared to catch that necklace the first chance I got.

"I don't know what the hell you're even talking about!" the man said, raising his voice. "You need to back up!"

"I don't need to do *shit*!" Wurthers argued back. "You asked for it, and you're gonna get it!"

"Is that right?" his opponent said. "Show me then, show me that your short ass can actually hit something above yo—"

He was instantly cut off again by a brutish blow to the jaw. He recoiled back in pain and gave Wurthers a death stare. He fired back, throwing a fist into Wurthers' face but missing it as Wurthers moved barely in time. The attack wasn't over; however, the man's elbow jutted out to the side and hit Wurthers in the ear. Both injured, they took defensive stances and prepared to make another move against each other. Trapped on the edge of the fight, I was weaving around the flying body parts and barely dodging the cheering crowd.

Multiple blows were made, and so few landed. Wurthers got a fist to the nose, causing a nosebleed, but the other man was bleeding from his mouth. His jaw had taken multiple hits from the short aggressor, likely enough to be broken.

Abruptly, the defender made a fake-out and then launched a kick at Reese, thrusting him to the ground and knocking the wind out of him. This was my chance. As quick as I could, I reached down to his collar once again and snagged the necklace without making contact with his skin. The necklace instantly disappeared in a cloud of black dust, followed by a faint screech only I could hear. I never got to see what the necklace looked like, but I was relieved to have won.

I got my hand out of the situation just in time for Wurthers to regain his thoughts and get back up for more. He threw his silky silver hair out of his face and charged at his opponent. He was knocked back again with a backhand to the face, followed by grabbing his loose hand and slamming him to the ground once again. Wurthers didn't freeze up and exhale smoke at all; his insides weren't incinerated! This meant a fun and entertaining death for the records. I very much looked forward to watching it. Perhaps it would be in the fight I was witnessing.

Wurthers started coughing up blood, but he kept attempting to strike back. He was moving slower, and his enemy took advantage of it. As time went on, the crowd was still glued to the fight, continuously trapping me inside. Realizing I could simply leap out of the crowd, I jumped to the sky and landed only a few feet away from the group of bystanders.

About to watch the fight from a safe distance, I noticed an irregularly large new army of people approaching, seemingly teenagers. Confused, I let them all walk by and observed their numbers. They made their way to the fight and began to move people out of their way.

"Reese!" the leader cried out.

The fight suddenly ended, Wurthers down on his knees again. The man he picked a fight with backed away, placing himself within the crowd of watchers. Wurthers picked himself up and spoke blood.

"What the hell do you guys want?" he said. "Can't you tell I'm busy right now?"

"Busy with what, getting your ass handed to you?" the leader said. The entire sea of people laughed and snickered at this, especially the newly arrived teenagers.

"You wanna piece of me, too?!" Reese yelled. "I've beaten all your asses before, and I'll do it again!"

"Think you can take on all of us?" the leader said back. "We've got everyone that you've used and abused, and we're ready to stand our ground."

"You're out of your mind, Sherman. You wouldn't dare—"

Sherman took a fast step forward before stopping himself. Wurthers flinched and backed away with a frightened expression on his face. Sherman smiled at this and made the full commitment. He pledged his fist to the right eye of Reese Wurthers and chucked him to the ground for the hundredth time.

The large group of teenagers chimed in and formed a circle around Reese, beating the blood out of him. The mindless hivemind aggression only hastened, and soon the cheering from the outside crowd disappeared and was turned into gasps and exclamations. Some even turned and walked away.

Soon, screams were made, and the clique of hostile teens slowly backed away from their former bully. I let out a laugh as the beaten body of Reese Wurthers was revealed. His face and arms were covered in blood, limbs violently shaking and quivering. He turned on his back, and vomit mixed with blood erupted from his gaping mouth. The bully victims started to panic as the public began to scream more and fly away.

Reese's body stiffened with an abrupt stop and let out the death shudder before going limp. Reese Wurthers was dead.

The teens fell like dominoes; each one of them scattered away and darted away from the crime scene. Laughing at the terrifying situation, I approached the dead teenager and took a quick look at his brutal injuries. His body was mangled and destroyed. I saw the irony in his death, but I wished it was bloodier.

"Everybody gets more than what they deserve, given time," I spoke aloud in a soliloquy. "What you deserved was not an early end, but a violent end."

I walked back to my bloodportal, still laughing at the horrific end of Wurthers. As I neared the portal, I heard the sirens of police cars approach. They would not share the same amusement as I did.

The authorities arrived at the scene just as I reached my destination. They put their hands to their heads, chins, and hips, eyeing the bludgeoned corpse. I let out one last chuckle before ripping open the bloodportal and stepping inside.
***

I ended up back on the road, where I crashed Whitewinter's car. The totaled car was gone already, even though I had only been gone for a short time. Knowing where to go, I started walking back to the house I broke out of. Satisfied with the end of Whitewinter's contract, I cheerfully walked all along the side of the road.

It only took an hour to arrive back at the house. There was a tow truck parked in the driveway, letting me know I didn't have to wait for Whitewinter to take his sweet time getting back home. I took a glance at the wall I punctured, seeing Monroe sitting down and hanging his feet out of it. Once he caught me approaching, he jumped up and ran back inside.

I leaped up to the hole and landed in the bedroom of Rodney Whitewinter once again. The two were waiting for me, expressions of fear and anxiety painting their faces like a canvas. I scoffed at their emotions and spoke to them.

"Wurthers is dead. Your soul belongs to the Devil now," I said, grinning sinisterly. "One day you will join the millions of souls being endlessly tortured in a lake of fire."

Rodney suddenly broke down and began to weep. Monroe put an arm around his shoulder, trying desperately to comfort him. He nodded to me, telling me I could finally go. I began to silently laugh to myself, walking to the bloodportal on the floor. Looking below it, I noticed their dare of a ritual was poorly made, so much so that I was taken aback by the fact it worked.

I suddenly stopped myself before going in and turned my eyes to the dismembered body of Brad, still lying on the floor in pieces. The gold-and-silver watch was still attached to his arm, and its gleam called my name.

I walked to the corpse and picked up the severed arm, trying to detach it. I growled as I struggled. This watch was precious! It was a sign of wealth and power to the bully of Brad. For me, it'd be not just a fancy trophy, but a symbol of power as well. It showed my bitter ruthlessness and the potential my hands could create! It showed that even the rich could be a victim by my hand!

Still struggling, I gave up on attempting to slip it off and instead slipped the entire arm into my satchel. Working to make it fit, I snapped it in half, spraying more blood on my hands. Carefully, I set it snugly between my other trophies of kills, where it fit perfectly.

I turned around to see Rodney still burying his head in his arms. He was utterly miserable, and I enjoyed watching. Monroe sat with him, saying nothing as Rodney cried. My contract was done.

Chapter Five

Pebbles crunching beneath my feet, I landed back in my spot in Hell. Next to the throne of Satan, I knew there wasn't a way to sneak past again. The humid air tensed my nerves like a knotted rope. The amount of trouble I was in was considerably dangerous... I knew I could get out of it, but I must choose my words carefully. Punishment was inevitable.

I took one step toward the path leading away from the throne before stopping. A long, deep breath escaped my mouth, and I slouched my head to the floor. I knew what was coming. Prolonging it was useless.

I resumed walking, heading out to the stone bridge, where I could clearly be seen by the Devil. As the seconds passed by, the eerie silence only turned my anxiousness up. It's not like Satan to be completely silent.

As I reached the stone bridge, my molten heart started pounding faster and faster. Slowly, I rotated my head around to see the throne. I could not even try to leave without speaking to Satan. The more I avoided him, the more trouble I'd be in.

Lucifer was indeed present. His eyes were fixed

upon me, and his upper lip was twitching. The lava flowing from his skin was like the rapids on Earth: fast, deadly, and intimidating. His heavy breathing was being restrained by the slimmest sense of self-control. My guts felt like they were being crushed the way I was being stared down.

"Lucifer!" I yelled, putting on the world's worst fake smile. "I got that contract done, pretty fast, too. Listen, I know what you're thinking, but you have to hear me out. I, eh... It wasn't against the rules!"

Satan's scowl grew more frustrated the more I spoke. His eyes were ablaze, chock full of insanity. His silence was the loudest voice one could hear...palpable and fear-inducing.

"Ah...my lord?" I said, mildly shaking while finally kneeling down. "Is there anything else you need from me? I'm, uh...I'm not busy..."

"You...pestilent, ignorant, reckless, foolish rat!" he muttered behind clenched teeth. "You just couldn't help yourself, could you?"

"Satan, I— He has forsaken us! Me and you and the other Hellstitchers!" I complained.

"And what?!" he yelled, finally blowing up. "You had a job to do, and you let the beliefs of some unworthy and unimportant human decide your next move?! I should raze you where you stand! You killed a human without any permission, and you did so without a second thought! You think his opposing beliefs gave you the power to do such a thing?!"

"Well...I—" I started.

"No, Decipere!" he interrupted. "I have the power! *I* do! You cannot kill people unless you are instructed to!"

"Our rules say nothing about killing other humans!" I yelled back. "I realize you don't like it when I *do*, but I haven't done it in over six decades! Six decades! Do you have any idea how good it feels to dismember whoever I like? It's like a drug! And not having it for so long has starved me. I'm like a rabid animal!"

Satan scoffed and leaned in closer. The lava falls began to slow down, and his teeth were no longer clenched.

"I am your potentate. Whatever I say goes, and that's that," he said. "No more killing. Or I will kill YOU!!"

Instantly, my body stood up on its own, and my teeth gritted against one another. I was so close to losing all control... I needed my vengeance, and I needed it now. There's no telling how lost my mind would be if I didn't get it anytime soon.

"I am going to reforge the Hellstitchers' rules, as a reminder," Satan resumed, leaning back into his throne. "I don't have a contract for you. Now leave me."

I stood in silence and looked to the floor. My enlarged fingers were twitching, close to snapping. My dazzling red eyes were blind; everything was processing inside my head. When I finally looked back up, the Devil was rubbing his temples, muttering incomprehensible words.

Stepping away, I too began to mutter. Setting my sights back on the stone bridge, I found Atrocify waiting for me. He was leaning against a cobbled pillar with his arms crossed. I rolled my eyes and began to walk his way.

Atrocify was my second-in-command. He's loyal,

intelligent, and could put up a fight. None that I lost, of course. If I wasn't the Monger, it'd certainly be him. Demons had spread rumor about his skill as a Hellstitcher being equal to mine, but there's a clear difference. The work I did had no equal, and I made sure of it. My methods and strategies were the best of the best. Atrocify could only hope to know them.

"Don't speak a word," I said, reaching the bridge.

"We need to talk, Decipere," he replied. "Me, you, and the other Hellstitchers."

"I already have plans to head for the Library of the Damned," I argued. "Can't it wait?"

"That's where the others are," Atrocify said, starting up a stride. "Come on, it's important."

I let out an audible sigh and began walking alongside him. Honestly, I'd rather be doing another contract than talking to the others. I had no time for fools who were poor at their jobs, especially Tenebris. What importance could this conversation hold?

"What is this about? Why is it so important?" I asked, rolling my eyes again.

"It's about you, Decipere," Atrocify answered. "And it's important because it'll help us work in unity."

"What is that supposed to mean?"

"You'll find out soon, Monger. For now, let's just get to our destination. All the talk we do is supposed to be with the others, not between you and me."

"I don't have the patience for this! I could be working on another contract..." I complained.

"Tenebris is the only one with a contract right now! And it's best if he is not told of this discussion."

I stopped and paused for a moment, thinking. If Tenebris had to be kept out of this...then what could be going on? I wondered if he had been gaining Satan's favor. Perhaps Satan wished for him to succeed me...

"Why?" I quietly asked.

"Keep walking," Atrocify said, still striding along.

A grunt came out of me as I resumed my walk with Atrocify. We walked in a dooming silence; the only noise in Hell came from the still-sleeping demons. Their snoring was faint yet frightening. Not to me, of course. I was the mighty Monger; fear was like a fantasy to me.

A long walk later, we arrived at the Library of the Damned. The entrance was built into the cave wall of Hell and was guarded by four demons, not that this place needed guarding anyway. The Silent Librarian was a powerful being in and of herself, and she needed no extra defense to keep herself safe.

When Atrocify and I entered, we were instantly greeted by the smell of rotting flesh. The entrance hall walls were decorated with torches ablaze, fueled by the extra souls the Librarian kept for herself. The interior was only small and compact for now, but when opening into the real library itself, it was like a maze. Faintly, one could hear the sounds of screaming, if they were silent enough. It was a pleasant sound, a comforting sound. It was one that eased the mind and put worries to rest.

The Librarian stood upon her perch, watching us as we approached. She lifted a hand without a word and beckoned us to her doorway. Silent ourselves, we made our way to the doors of the library. When we arrived, the Librarian reached out her hand and demanded our payment.

"Do you have anything to pay with?" Atrocify

whispered.

"Yeah. I do," I whispered back, reaching my hand into my satchel. Stealthily, I pulled out the arm I had just got only a half-hour ago. With a loud *SNAP*, I broke it into two pieces and put the forearm part back into my satchel. Blood squirted over the clean, cut-stone floor, the Librarian giving me a disapproving look.

"Decipere, are you serious?" Atrocify said, a little louder than a whisper this time. "You're making a mess of her home."

"It's all I have," I argued. "Besides, she likes bigger limbs more than the puny fingers and toes you guys give her."

"Yeah? Maybe you're right, Decipere, but they still work just as well," he replied with a hint of sass. "She certainly doesn't mind it when they're coming from me."

Atrocify snatched the broken arm from my hand and piled it in with his handful of severed fingers. He shoved it into the Librarian's hand and opened the doors, disappearing into the library. I followed, allowing the creaky hinges to close the door behind me.

The steamy air of the library burned hotter than the normal fumes of Hell. The hotter it was in here, the more souls were being kept. Luckily for us, souls that rested here were damned for an eternity. Not a single human left without God pulling them out himself, and he hadn't done so in years.

While this was a place I enjoyed, it required payment every hour I dwelled there. Flesh and bones were what the Librarian liked, so it was flesh and bones we gave. It's not difficult to get said payment, but we couldn't get too much before Satan took it away.

Strolling along the edges of the Sanguine River, Atrocify and I made our way to the other Hellstitchers, who were already busy torturing a poor young boy's soul. The boy was weeping and squirming on the ground, while Immolatus was carving his name into the boy's back with his cudgel. Gomorrah was sitting on the ground, taunting the boy. What a joke this was.

"Hellstitchers!" I barked.

The demons immediately turned their attention to me and knelt down to their knees. Atrocify tossed the boy back into the river after realizing he was about to make a run for it. Screams of horror erupted from the boy as he was slowly being pulled down back into the depths of the bloody river. Shrieks slowly faded, until only the scared silence replaced them.

"Monger, we've been waiting," Immolatus said with an upmost professional tone.

"I can see that..." I said back. "And instead of waiting patiently, you two chose to fool around."

Immolatus shot up like a bullet, an enraged expression painting his face.

"Well, we wouldn't be messing around if you didn't piss off Satan and get sent on another contract!" he roared, pointing a bony finger. "If you just did your job and stopped complaining about it like the rest of us, we would be in a lot better shape, and we'd even have a better leader at that!"

"If you want to debate leadership then let's talk it out in the arena!" I argued. "Personally, I don't like being a kiss-ass to our sire Satan, unlike the ignorant fool that is you."

He took a step forward and immediately took it back, knowing he wouldn't stand a chance fighting it out. His yellow glare belonged to a child, one that could never think for himself. His mind was set on being Lucifer's little teacher's pet, despite him not having any ounce of freedom out of it.

"Why do you make this a habit, Decipere?" Atrocify interrupted. "You *are* a good leader, but picking fights with everyone is not going to get you anywhere. You're the toughest demon in Hell, everyone knows that, so you don't have to keep trying to prove it."

"Yes, I do," I whispered with a grit. "It's up to me to make sure no one forgets their place."

"But that's Satan's job!" Gomorrah suddenly cried out. "He's the big boss! No one else tell him what to do!"

I bit my tongue for a minute. Satan's rule wouldn't be in effect for much longer, but I couldn't tell the other Hellstitchers of my beliefs; I'd be dead. Even Atrocify could rat me out; his loyalties belonged more to Satan than they did to me. Not that I had any ideas on how to usurp him in the first place...

"Gomorrah," I began, "watch what you say. I still have authority over every lost soul in this doomscape. Nothing changes that. Satan won't make the effort to show everyone who's boss, but I sure will. He's too busy sitting in his chair, watching the humans of Earth fiddle with their lives. Useless."

"He's not just sitting there and watching. He's trying to tempt them," Atrocify said. "If it wasn't for him, we wouldn't get nearly as many contracts as we do."

An audible scoff came out of me. I considered saying something snarky back, but we're already wasting my time. I needed to get answers quickly so I could get the others out of my hair.

"Fine," I said. "What do you guys want, anyway?"

Atrocify looked to Immolatus and nodded. Immolatus returned a nod and spoke.

"Decipere, you are aware Tenebris is a part of our race, right?"

"Yeah, what about it?" I asked back.

"The Devil may be making another Hellstitcher, and he'll be replacing one of us. If he makes it, he wants to replace the worst of us. Obviously, you, the Monger, have nothing to worry about."

"Why is he getting a new one?" I demanded. "The contest already decided us five as the best."

"Yeah, in battle prowess," he replied with sass. "We're the five best warriors, sure, but that doesn't mean we're good at the one job that we live for."

"We still get the job done, right? So why the hell does it matter?"

"It matters because the more humans are aware of our existence, the more we risk extinction! Would you do such a sloppy job that it gets suspicious enough for the world to hunt us down? In unison? We don't know if they can obtain a power to kill us!"

"We need humans to be aware!" I said, raising my voice. "That's the only way we can get contracts!"

"They can't be so aware of us that some want to find a way to kill us..." he whispered. "I'll bet there are already a few humans trying to find a way. Earth will never bow down to us in unison. There's always going to be some who are against us. That's the way it is."

"I see... And with God as their ally, he's not going to let us get away with a mass slaughter."

"Right. And, back to the point, we need to be prepared to lose one of our members," he said in a tamer tone. "Decipere, in case Tenebris is chosen, we need you to treat him with the respect that he deserves. We're supposed to be honorable, and your actions against him are atrociously disgusting."

"He doesn't deserve my respect!" I growled. "A poor worker he is, and an equally poor warrior. I won't respect that."

"He is a Hellstitcher!" Immolatus snapped back. "He deserves as much respect as the rest of us, and you're too busy giving him shit for being weaker than you!"

"Yeah, he'll always be that way," I said with a smug smile. "He's trying too hard to be me, the Monger. He thinks he's special enough to fill a role that he's just not cut out for."

"He's not trying to take your place, Decipere," Atrocify butted in. "He's trying to impress you. We, as Hellstitchers, although demonic, are like brothers to each other. Tenebris thinks of you as the big brother; he wants your attention."

"Do—don't make jokes," I said, holding back a chuckle. "He's not human. He can't think of me like that."

"He does. We've been made to kill by exploiting a weakness every human has, but that doesn't mean we don't have that weakness, too. Tenebris holds sentiment to you."

"I don't believe you. If he thinks of me like that, he wouldn't be such a thorn in the side. He's an asshole."

"Only because you choose to think of him as so. If you changed your way of thinking, you could turn him into a friend. Of course, if he's the one who gets replaced, he'll die knowing he meant something to you."

"Yes, and that something is a vermin."

Atrocify's exhausted look turned into disappointment as he rubbed his fingers onto his temple.

"Decipere, just..." he started. "He looks up to you. Act like a mentor. Even if you train him well, he still won't ever be better than you. You know this."

"Hmpf!" I grunted. "I'll consider it."

"Good," Immolatus said. "Gomorrah, let's get out of here."

"Souls to torture!" Gomorrah shrieked, reaching into the Sanguine River. "More souls to torture, still!"

"No!" Immolatus snapped. "We've been here for hours! We're leaving."

Swiftly, he yanked Gomorrah by the chains wrapping around his torso and pulled him away from the river. Groans and pouts leaked from Gomorrah's mouth as the two slowly strode away. I rolled my eyes and opened my satchel, wanting to get away from the sour conversation.

"Observe, Atrocify," I spoke. "This is a trophy from the boy I killed, a gold watch that symbolizes wealth."

"It's...eh, wonderful. What are you going to do with it?"

"I'm going to keep it inside my bag. Every time I open it up, it'll remind me that nothing escapes my grasp, not even the rich."

A sigh came from under his breath before he walked away in disgust. His hand beckoned me to follow, as if to tell me I was in trouble. We walked together once more, this time leading out of the library. We said nothing to each other as we bid farewell. A sense of anger swelled up inside as I watched him sluggishly walk away. I was losing his respect, faster than I could think. I needed to correct it.

Hands twitching, I began walking his way. I would remind him that it was me who deserved respect! If he wouldn't give that to me, he'd surely pay for it. I had Atrocify in my sights, just a few meters away. I walked faster, flesh burning from the magma-like ground.

Just as my hand reached his shoulder, the Devil blew his horn. A new contract was open. Atrocify gave a cold stare as I kept my hand connected to him. A jaded moment of silence passed before either of us broke.

"Do you want that one?" he asked.

"Yes," I replied without a second thought. I immediately broke into a sprint along the stony road. I passed Gomorrah on the way, much to his dismay. He hadn't gotten to do a contract in weeks, but it's not a problem of mine.

Reaching the throne panting, I bent down to my knee and extended my hand out.

"Lucifer!" I coughed before clearing my throat. "I have come for the next contract. Who am I working for?"

"Decipere. Who did you push out of the way to get here first?" he said in a disappointed tone.

"The asylum patient, sire."

"Oh." He chuckled. "Your contractor's last name is Gomez; he lives in the United States of America."

He handed me a withered scroll, containing all the information I needed. The place I was going to was Arizona, a terribly hot and arid state. There wasn't a lot to say about it, but the cacti were a wonder to see for everyone.

My bloodportal made an audible splat as it appeared behind me. Closing my eyes and cooling off, I swiftly ripped it open and took a leap inside.

***

Blasting out of the bloodportal, I landed in the middle of an RV. The seats were folded back just enough to make the ritual work, and the bed was forcibly taken out of the vehicle. I felt the tips of my horns pierce the weak roof, and I uttered a groan of frustration. Before me was a man standing strong. He had the look of determination splattered all over him. This was Gomez.

"Hellstitcher," he said, barely moving an inch. "You are here to kill whomever I choose, for the price of my soul, correct?"

"Hahaha...yeah." I laughed. "Enjoy damnation. There's no going back."

"Yes, I know. Before I give you the name, I want to make it clear that I do not agree with this."

"Yeah?" I scoffed at him. "Then why are you doing it?"

"I'm sure you'll find out," he harshly whispered.

My smile melted and turned to a glare. This man was not like the usual douchebags I ran into. He was focused.

"Just give me the name, whelp," I demanded.

"Right, his name. Of course..." he softly said back.

Chapter 6

DRIVEN

A sort of doctor, this man was. Highly skilled in the technology field. My curiosity as to why Gomez wanted this man dead was eating away at my consciousness. He didn't want a Hellstitcher, yet he called one anyway. The words he said shrouded his intentions with mystery, only gatekeeping the interesting bits.

Regardless of my curiosity, I had a job to do. This doctor was a few states away, and a bloodportal was awaiting me. The scent he gave off was strong; I could tell this contract was going to be somewhat unique.

Leaping through the portal, and a splash of horrendous blood later, I landed on the soft grass below. The fertile ground felt relaxing on my feet; the blades were gently caressing them like a massage from an angel. Across the yard, a small house stood firm. It was alone and surrounded by trees. One cheapskate car sat in the driveway. The doctor was inside.

I quickly made my way to the door and phased myself inside. A delightful scent waved through the air, much different from most of the previous victims' households. A small kitchen loomed to the left side, with a living room to my right. Only a hallway stood in front of me.

Subtly making my way through the house, I first explored the kitchen. The countertop was immaculately clean. There were no dirty dishes in sight, and it looked as though it was brand new.

"Daddy, are you ready yet?" a voice cried out. A little girl, absolutely, but where did it come from?

I stepped out of the kitchen into the dining room. Nothing. I went to step back into the kitchen before something caught my eye. A framed photograph, mounted on the dining room wall. I leaned closer to make sure I saw what I thought I saw.

It was Gomez, with his arm around a lab-coated man, who was bringing in both Gomez and another fellow. This doctor was friends with Gomez... But why did he want the man dead?

My mind racing, I rushed out of the dining room and kitchen and made my way into the living room. There, sitting on the floor, was a child. She was coloring a picture by herself. As I gradually moved closer, I could tell what it was. Four figures stood side by side: a fox, a chicken, a bear, and a purple rabbit. The bear had a microphone, and the rabbit held a poorly drawn guitar. She was making a band out of animals.

"Daddy!" she yelled out again.

"Yes, I'm ready, Munchkin. Just hold on another minute," a deep voice returned to her.

I knew he was here. His scent had gotten incredibly powerful. All I needed to do now was observe. When the next day arrived, I shall strike him down where he stood, and I would find out why he needed to die.

The man finally stepped out of the door. His bald head shined brighter than any star I'd seen, and his formal lab coat wore high status and skill. A silvery boxed beard stood out from his face, as well as a thick pair of glasses. For a moment, as he looked to his daughter, he paused and looked in my direction. A question burned in my head, asking if he saw me... As impossible as that was, the feeling crept up on me like a cat watching its prey.

"Daddy!" the girl cried, leaping to her feet. She threw herself into the doctor's arms, almost staggering him.

"Hey, Munchkin," he started. "Are you gonna play with your friends while I'm at work?"

"Yeah!" she replied with a grin. "You want me home at the same time again?"

"That would be great..." he said while letting go. He strode to the door and grabbed his keys off a rack, turning back to his daughter.

"I'm coming," she said while picking up her drawing. She placed it on the wooden stained coffee table and raced to the door.

Together, they walked out and locked the door behind them. I looked around the house to see if there were any more objects that stood out, but there was nothing of note. It was a plain house; there was nothing of interest anywhere you looked. This contract may be of some difficulty, but there's always something to love.

Moving quickly, I phased out of the house to see the two hugging one last time.

"Hey, don't get into anything you're not supposed to," the doctor said.

"Uhh...got it. I love you, Daddy!"

"I love you, too, Munchkin. Go mess around."

He squeezed her one last time before letting go. She took off only a second later, running on a dirt path that led behind the house. After that, she disappeared.

I looked back at the old man to see him walking to his car. He showed no sign of knowing my presence. That was only normal; there was no reality where he knew I was here. My discomfort a few minutes ago was unjustified.

Still, as a matter of fact, I felt I needed to make sure. As he walked to his car, I jogged my way up and stuck my foot out in front of him. Completely oblivious, it seemed, he tripped right over me. A grunt later and he fell to the ground, knees and hands covered in soil.

"Gah..." he whimpered.

I chuckled at his discomfort. Even the slightest of "accidents" could make my day. If he knew I was here, he'd have no trouble avoiding my trap. Suspicion averted.

On the other hand, though, if he really did know I was here, perhaps he walked into me on purpose. Could he really be playing dumb? Was I the one being toyed with? These thoughts were clawing at my mind, as if they were wild animals. If I continued to doubt myself, I'd go as crazy as Gomorrah.

The man did nothing to clean himself off. Instead, he simply continued his walk to the car. After getting in, he did what any human would do: start the car and drive off. How entertaining...

As minutes passed, I ran alongside the road, following my target. For a while, I assumed his work was only going to be a few minutes away, but I was being proven quite wrong. I took my Rolex arm out of my satchel and realized it'd already been over an hour since we hit the road. If I had to watch this man for another day, I may just destroy his whole house to kill him.

At long last, we reached a building. The parking lot was colossal; its pavement reached a solid two hundred feet on both sides of the entrance. The building read "Sol's Technologies" on the front. I'd never been in a place like this. It'd surely be as interesting as this world got, but my job wasn't to be a tourist.

The doctor and I entered the facility. Various rooms decorated the entire space. Each room seemed to be testing their own unique items. One room had scientists and men in suits gathered around a massive table, discussing matters beyond me. This whole building was a wonder.

Not paying any attention to the path in front of me, I ran into another scientist. He fell to the ground and dropped a cup of coffee, making a stench of a mess.

"Shit," I uttered. I stood out of the way and quickly made my way to the wall.

"Are you all right, Donny?" the doctor said to him, helping him to the ground.

"I— Eh... No, I—" Donny stuttered. "I swear I walked into something, but th-there wasn't anything there!"

"You know, the invisible walling lab is in the south wing," the doctor replied. "Their products shouldn't be ending up in here."

Donny stuck an arm out and reached in front of him, trying to grab my now-moved wall of a body. He couldn't make contact with anything. The doctor shook his head and continued on his way.

"Maybe you should see a counselor!" he shouted.

Donny looked back with a gaping mouth and realized his coffee was splattered on the floor. The mixed expressions coming off his face were priceless. I laughed and walked away, back to the doctor. I should have knocked him over on purpose.

As the day dragged on, I oversaw a rather boring day of this doctor. Just an average day at work, nothing real interesting, outside of the projects going on in other rooms. It just so happened that my guy was working on a new casual clothing that was completely fireproof yet still mimicked the qualities of normal clothes. I disliked when things could not be destroyed with fire.

After a sleep-inducing eight hours, the doctor finally shut his computer off. He put a few items into a closet and headed out the door.

"Hey, wait!" a coworker yelped.

The doctor peered back into the room with a curious expression.

"I really like your new glasses," she said. "I thought you got a new pair only a month ago?"

"Ah, I was so unsatisfied with them," he said with a smile. "My eye doctors are very understanding."

"Yeah, nice..." she said awkwardly.

"Good night," the doctor said as he walked back out the door.

The woman felt disturbing to be around. She

certainly had feelings for the doctor, but she couldn't express them for the life of her.

I walked out as well, only a few seconds behind the old man. As I followed him home, I finally felt the joy of stalking again. Being cramped up in that lab was torturous; I swore I almost fell asleep a dozen times. The run back to the house was equally uneventful, but it let me feel the wind on my horns again.

Arriving home, the doctor hastily made his way inside and left the door swinging wide open. Curiously, I walked inside, still having to phase myself through the entrance. Odd leaving his door open... Perhaps his daughter was arriving home as well. As I walked through the house again, I heard the doctor rummaging through drawer of sorts, and then he spoke.

"If you wouldn't mind, can you close my front door?" he said with a firm voice.

Who was this man talking to? There was no one else in the house. No one except for me. But I assumed he didn't know I was here...

"Yes, I'm talking to you, Hellstitcher," he said again. "I know you're here."

"I—" I started.

The doctor walked into the living room, where I was standing, looked directly into my eyes, and spoke again.

"Close the door, please," he told me.

I growled and spoke back to him.

"Make me, human."

A scoff came from the man, as he began walking to the front door. I didn't move an inch. Hundreds of thoughts ran through my mind as I heard the door close. The doctor came back into the living room and gleefully took a seat on his couch.

"Um, I made these contacts..." he began. "They allow me to see your kind and to hear them. They're full of technology beyond the average scientist. We don't study these kinds of things, demons, but I, as an individual, do."

"Wonderful," I said sternly.

"Yes, it is wonderful," he said back. "I have goals, Hellstitcher. These contacts are a cog in the machine to reach those goals."

"It'd be a shame if they were destroyed," I said, finally turning my wretched head to him. Rage filled my blood. I wanted to snap every bone in this man's body.

"Yeah, no, I agree. I, eh... They can't really be destroyed. I work with a company, as you saw, that invents numerous things. I was allowed to use some tech to come up with these contacts. Completely indestructible, they are. Fireproof, too, in case you wanted to heat them up. I imagine it'd also be fairly difficult to pull them off of me."

"I'll stab your eyes out!" I suddenly yelled, fists clenched.

"Don't do that, Hellstitcher. You may just end up killing me. I'm very much an oldie, and you must understand my health is not in the best condition. I know you don't want that to happen..."

I said nothing but only growled.

"So here's what's going to happen. I have a weapon. It's incomplete as of now but will be usable within a few days. My friend, Gomez, didn't have the time to summon you after his move, so we had to make do with this day. Your job is to kill me, but you cannot, for I have nothing I love inside this house."

Shit. This man knew too much; I had to kill him as soon as I could. If the Devil found out about this man, maybe he could make an exception for the rules.

"What's the weapon for? To kill me?" I asked.

"Uh...yeah. To kill you and your entire group of Hellstitchers. There are five of you, right? Including the Monger?"

"Why are you asking if you already know?" I said with a smirk. My attitude had just changed dramatically. If he sought to kill the Hellstitchers, he'd need me to help him. I wondered if this weapon actually worked... I wondered if I could use it to kill Satan...

"Just making sure, that's all!" he replied, getting defensive. "Anyway, I need you to give me a few days before anything happens. I know you only have a week, but I assure you it'll be done. Besides, perhaps I'll let you live, and you'll only be demoted to a normal demon status in Hell. Also, I want to remind you again, and make it very clear, you won't be able to kill me."

"Why's that?"

"I already told you, Hellstitcher. I hold sentimental value to a grand total of zero things within this house. I'd be surprised if you found something outside the house, too. You kill by destroying things people love, right? Why is that?"

"Why is that? It's to exploit the weakness every human has: they care for at least one thing in this world. It's quite...hellish, to lose things you love."

"I agree. That's why I only love my daughter. You

cannot kill her. I know full well you can't."

"Right. Well, what else do you want to blabber on about? Do you want me to answer any more questions? Because I'm sure you already know more than you need."

Chapter Seven

OPPORTUNIST

"Do you want to know what I really want, Hellstitcher?" the doctor asked, seemingly bored of the conversation. "What I really *need*?"

"Not really," I said. "But I've got time to listen."

The doctor smiled before putting a stern face on and leaning forward on his couch. His dark brows furrowed as he froze his laser eyes onto mine.

"I need the Monger first," he said. "He's the most dangerous out of all of them. The smartest, the strongest, and the fastest. The odds of you being the Monger are about one out of five, right? Assuming there are still five of you Hellstitchers?"

"Yeah, sure," I said with a blank expression.

"Well, are you the Monger? Am I gonna have to kill you first? When the time comes, I mean."

An idea sprung into my head. If this old man could really kill a Hellstitcher, it could not be me. Perhaps, if he worked more, he could make a Satan-killing weapon... What if that's possible? I needed to test his Hellstitcher weapon first to make sure of it. Maybe I could even take it and kill the other Hellstitchers once the Devil was dead. The chance had come, and the plan was brewing.

"Fortunately for me, no, I'm not the Monger," I started. "The title of Monger belongs to an incompetent fool by the name of Tenebris."

"Okay...and you are?" he asked hesitantly.

"Decipere," I answered with confidence. "I am what you could call a 'second in command.' The right hand of the Monger."

"So I should kill you next, then?"

"I wouldn't prefer that. I'm hardly better than any of the other Hellstitchers. In fact, I was chosen second in command simply because my powers are better than the others."

"How humble of you to say that," the doctor said. "But how can I trust you're telling the truth? You are a demon. For all I know, this could be a ploy, a trick to get me to kill you last. Or to buy you time to think of an escape."

"Well, because, Baldy, I want the Monger dead, too," I said with a growl. "Perhaps more than *you* want him dead."

He had to bite onto this. Just a little more convincing, and he may believe me. The odds were in my favor; they had to sway my way.

"Yeah? I heavily doubt that," he said with an offended tone.

"Right, well, I'm going to let you in on something you probably already know," I said with a slight whisper before letting out a bellow. "The Monger is a revolting slob! He bears no right to hold his title, and he doesn't do half a job as the rest of us do! The lazy and incompetent bastard is reveling in his glory, while the rest of us Hellstitchers get to watch on the bench! I'd gladly lead him to you. I'd gladly watch him die. Maybe one of us could actually make use of the title."

A silent pause came from the doctor as he

looked to the side and stroked his beard. His deep thought was interrupted by my grunt, nudging him for a reply.

"Do you think *you* deserve the title?" the doctor finally asked.

"I do, and I'd love being the Monger," I said. "However, the same could be said for every one of us. Like I said, the only advantage I have over the others are my powers."

"Okay, okay. Forget I asked that," he started. "You're really hellbent on getting rid of him, then?"

"That is correct."

"And if you were the only one left, you'd be the only one capable of being the Monger, am I right?"

"You're right," I replied with haste. "Actually...I'd like to make a deal with you."

"You're not making the shots, Decipere. I am."

"Hear me out, demon slayer. If you could help me become the Monger, I'll lure my brothers to you, and I won't even make an attempt to kill you."

The doctor paused again. He opened his mouth before quickly closing it again. He thought long and hard about my "deal." The anticipation was growing on me, though. I needed an answer from him. I needed to confirm his confidence in me.

"See, Decipere, I don't believe I can take your deal."

"Why is that?"

Suddenly, we heard the sound of the front door opening. A loud, "Daddy, I'm home!" echoed through the house. His daughter was home. Playtime may be over for today.

"Hey, Munchkin!" he yelled before turning to me

with a whisper. "We're not done here."

He swiftly jolted away and caught his daughter with a laugh. I let out a groan and turned away from the abhorrent sight. How could love be so powerful? It made little of sense to me. If I had love for anyone, I'd be limiting my own free will, and that was simply incomprehensibly disgusting.

"Hey, you got here right on time!" the doctor said with glee.

"Yeah! I'm really, really good at that!" his daughter said excitedly. She was so proud of herself.

I needed to know what time it was, too. I'd been out of Hell for longer than I needed to be, and I'd been stuck here talking to this wretched human for what seemed to be an eternity.

I searched for a clock on the wall, to no avail. I considered looking in the heavily decorated kitchen to find it on a stove before remembering I had a watch in my satchel. Pulling out the arm, I gazed at the expensive glittery watch still attached. It was six p.m. exactly.

"Today I played a lot with my friends at the park!" the little girl said as they moved into the living room. "We didn't get to go on the swings, though, because some bullies were hogging them."

"Did you ask them if you could have a turn?" the doctor said, coming into my vision. He looked at me in horrified shock as he turned his eyes to my location. I gazed at him with confusion before realizing I was still holding the human limb in my hand.

"Yeah, but they told us to go away," she continued as the doctor struggled to keep her looking away from my arm. I considered waving it around some more and scaring the light of day out of her, but I needed to play nice with Doc Brown for now. With only a moment's hesitation, I stuffed the arm back into my satchel and buttoned it closed so it didn't fall out with my lazy packaging.

The doctor glanced at me again and took a deep breath in relief. He turned back to his daughter and cleared his throat.

"Listen, Lila, I'm gonna tell you a little secret, okay?"

The girl rapidly shook her head up and down with a bright, mile-long smile across her face.

"Even though other kids can be stubborn, selfish brats, if you stand up for yourself enough, you can get what you want. It takes a lot of confidence, and a lot of bravery, but most kids are scared of starting fights, especially when they're in a public place, like a park. You just gotta tell them what you want. You wanted a turn on the swings, right? And if they still don't give you what you want, you can count on me to help you out a little, okay?"

"Okay!"

How insufferable.

"But! Let me remind you that it's a lot of power, being able to get help from an adult. And with great power comes great responsibility. Use that power wisely. I'm not always going to be able to help you. You're only eight, but you're gonna grow up pretty quickly, and responsibility is gonna follow you everywhere."

"Okay, Daddy," she said with the softest of tones.

"Now, you wanna have something special

tonight?" he asked.

"Yeah, what is it?" Lila asked with a smile.

"You, youngling, are going to get served dinner in your own bed."

"I get to eat in bed?"

"Yes, but only for tonight. I think I felt something odd come over me today."

"Okay! Yay!" she yelled, running over to her bedroom.

"You're gonna have to wait a bit before dinner is served, all right?" the doctor called.

"Okay!" Lila called back.

He waited a minute before sitting back down. He gave me a quick glance as he grabbed the picture Lila drew that was sitting on the coffee table.

"This is why I can't accept the deal," he said, showing me the drawing. "If there's still any one Hellstitcher alive, they're a liability to harm my daughter. If I leave you alive, you'll be forced to find some way to kill me, whether it'll be my daughter or not. I need to be there for her; she doesn't have anyone else."

I chuckled and rolled my eyes.

"Ah-ha, by the time the contract time limit is over, I'll have become the Monger," I said without hesitation. "A quite special perk of being the Monger is that I'd get to skip just one contract, as long as I returned the soul of whoever made it. That will be you and your pal Gomez."

"I never read that in my book," he said sternly.

"What book?" I asked hesitantly.

"I have a book, written by my mother. It's not important to you, only to me. She knows a lot about your kind."

"Clearly not enough," I said, squinting my eyes at the doctor.

"I guess so. Anyhow, I've only got one shot at this, so I need to know if this is true."

"If it wasn't true, I wouldn't have offered the deal in the first place. It wouldn't make sense. I'd be turned into a normal demon if that wasn't true. That's a fate worse than death," I said, desperately hoping he'd latch on.

"Decipere, if I leave you alive, and you inevitably don the title of the Monger, you swear to your allegiance to the Devil that no harm will come to me, my daughter, or Gomez?"

"I swear. I will lead the Monger to you. As for the other Hellstitchers, I will be the only Hellstitcher left," I said with an upright voice.

"Fine. You have a deal."

"Wonderful," I said with a sinister smile.

Victory, at least for now. The longer I kept this charade going, the better. As soon as I could confirm the weapon worked, I would take it and eliminate the Hellstitchers myself.

"This weapon of yours will be ready within a couple days you said, correct?" I asked.

"That's right, you should be able to keep yourself busy until then," he said. "Visit me in two days exactly, and when the time comes, don't let your overlord know you're luring the others."

"Got that, detective," I said snarkily.

"Let me warn you, too," he said, almost cutting me off.

"About what?"

"This weapon is the only one I have, and it took me years to perfect it. As powerful as it is, it is also vulnerable to being stolen."

"You think I'm going to steal your precious weapon?"

"I think it's always possible. But you don't have to worry. It will have a failsafe in case you *do* steal it. Just to…encourage you to keep your hands off."

"Let's hear it, then."

This wasn't good. I may have to cooperate with this man until the time came. If only being the Monger did have an option to skip a contract, I'd be home free. I needed to figure out my plan, as quickly as I could.

"It's a little, itty-bitty switch. Once flicked, it'll detonate the weapon, and every demonic force in the blast zone will instantly perish. You cannot reach the switch as well. It is protected from your kind."

"You've piqued my curiosity, Doc. You must be proud of this achievement."

"I am," he said with a smile. "Come, let me show you."

He guided me to the next room over: his bedroom. There were many knickknacks scattered about and lots of shelves full of gizmos and tools. One corner bore a desk and a computer, another some sort of case with a tarp over it. There was only one window, but its size was dwarfed by the sheer size of the room alone.

In a miniscule closet, there lay a pool of water, dug into the floor. One look down there told me there was a safe, only barely submerged below.

"Isn't it beautiful, Decipere?" the doctor asked, still smiling. "That is a different type of holy water.

Blessed by over one hundred priests of God. Can you believe I was able to do this?"

"Impressive," I said with a smirk. "Do you mind if I touch it?"

"Go ahead, I want to make sure you know this is real."

Slowly, I descended my right hand. I put out my smaller pinky finger to touch the smooth liquid. My heart beat faster the closer I got to it. If this was real, how in the hell was I going to get this safe? Even if I destroyed the flooring and ripped out the ground, the safe would be drenched in the stuff. Holy water didn't just evaporate, either; it'd easily stick to whatever came into contact with it. Except for the obvious odd one out: demons.

As my pinky barely touched the water's surface, I felt a searing sensation. It burned! Smoke erupted out of my pinky as I gripped it in pain, letting out a deep growl. Not good.

"Mhm. Just keep this moment in mind," the doctor said.

"Yeah, it'll be pretty difficult to forget, now that my finger will be throbbing for a week."

"Right. Well, now that we're on the same page, you have permission to go. Two days and my weapon will be ready. I don't want to keep you here any longer than I have to."

"I don't really want to be here any longer than I have to, either," I replied, still gritting my teeth.

"Until next time, then," he said, leaving the room. "Sorry, Lila, your dinner is just about ready now!"

As he left the room, I still stood at the closet,

staring at my roadblock. I gazed into the depths of the holy water, and my disgusted image gazed back. The safe was calling to me, yet I couldn't reach it. Rage swelled up in my body. No ideas came into mind; I was stuck.

What was I to do when Satan confronted me? I would have missed a contract, and my destiny would be crushed into bits. I couldn't be turned into a low-life demon... I'd rather die.

Time was of the essence. I needed to leave now and come up with something. If I did a contract when I got back, perhaps it'd ease my mind. It's the only thing I could do for now.

Making my way out of the house, I took one last look at the doctor's house. I could destroy it all right now; there's bound to be something here that the doctor cherished. I could do it, but I must restrain myself. Given this opportunity, solutions would have to be found. I turned away from the house and ran toward the portal. Taking a deep breath, I stepped through the blood.

***

Landing in my usual spot in Hell, I immediately walked up to the big throne. There Lucifer sat, nonchalantly smoothing out the molten lava over his arms. I cleared my fiery throat and got his attention.

"What do you want, Decipere? You haven't finished your contract yet!" he bellowed.

I kneeled down and spoke. "I know, sire. This one is seemingly quite difficult, even for me. I request another contract to help me clear my head."

"I have two available right now," he offered. "Are you sure you don't want the others to finally have a chance to do more contracts? They've been awfully hungry."

"Let them know I'll consider taking a break after this one," I said.

"Fine. You'll get a woman with the surname Foxx. She lives in Italy," he said with a frown. "Get out of here!"

A gruesome smile formed from my mouth as I left for my bloodportal again. I had two days. Just two days to think of something. This contract would surely ease my mind; it had to. My future, the tyrant of Hell, depended on it.

Chapter Eight

PATIENT

A dark area formed. The atmosphere was quiet, calm, and settled, lit only by a few strips of LED lights. I met the room of my next contractor. Heaps of clothes scattered the floor, and the walls were littered in fancy posters and decorations. Some were depicting my master, the Devil, in a buff, terrifying physique. Interest filled my thoughts, as my contractor was clearly a fan of Satan's works.

A young girl sat down in front of me. Covered in jet-black hair, she gazed at my person, awestruck by my appearance. At a moment's notice, I saw she had multiple piercings: one septum piercing, three studs on her ear, snakebites on her blackened lips, and one in her eyebrow.

I smirked at her shock and quickly began conversation.

"Miss Foxx?" I began. "I am your Hellstitcher. You will tell me the na—"

I was quickly cut off by the young girl's screeching excitement. With so many decibels, I could feel my eardrums trying to burst themselves open. I wanted to crush her windpipe before she was able to let out another scream.

"Oh em gee!" she cried. "I've been waiting forever

to meet you! I'm Emilia!"

She stuck out her hand with one rapid movement, asking for a handshake. Keeping my hands at my side, I let out a glare. How dare this whelp interrupt me!

"Put your hand away!" I yelled. "I am not here to be your friend. I'm here to kill someone!"

She dropped her arm and looked away with an awkward smile. She cleared her throat before pulling out a set of papers from behind her. I stood, confused as to why this girl was toying with me.

"Uh, Mr. Hellstitcher," she began, holding her finger up. "I am aware I summoned you to kill someone, but I want to ask you a few questions before I give you a name. That's not against the rules, is it?"

"No, but I don't—"

I stopped myself. I needed to keep my cool. What could go wrong if I stayed here for another minute or two? I only had two days.

"Grrrr, fine. Go ahead," I growled.

"Yay!" she yelled, focusing on the paper. "Okay, so first question: how long have you and your kind been alive?"

What a ridiculous question. Why was information like this important? There was no point in knowing this; all she could do was brag about it. Maybe that's the point.

"What could you possibly do with this information?" I demanded. "Tell your best pals?"

"I'm just curious! Maybe when I come down to Hell, I could, like, help you out and stuff!"

"That won't happen. You'll be stuck in the library for the rest of time."

"Well, maybe I can be an exception," she pleaded. "Can you just answer the question?"

"Hmph. We've been alive for maybe...two thousand years or so," I answered.

"'Kay, so... You've been doing this job your entire two-thousand-year life?"

"Almost," I replied hastily. "There were years dedicated to the coliseum days."

"...And?"

"And what?" I argued. "You want the full VIP access to the history of my race or something?"

"Uh, yeah?" she said. "Don't you think it's at least mildly interesting?"

"No. I lived it; I don't care to remember it."

"Why? Was it traumatizing?"

This question nearly split me open like a nut. I would not have my integrity and mental state challenged!

"I— No. It was not," I began, fists clenching. "I was a champion! I was the very best of the warriors. When the Devil grew bored two thousand years ago, he created an army of enhanced demons, which he called his 'Shadefighters.' We fought each other to the death and then revitalized as a loser. If you won, you rose through the ranks. I was at the top of the ranks! So how could I have been traumatized?"

"I dunno, maybe dying felt unbearable?" she said, clearly impatient with me. "So why are there only a few of you now?"

"The tournament," I started. "Humans summoning the Devil, asking him to kill people, in exchange for their souls. He didn't want to do all of the work, so he arranged a tournament. The five best

Shadefighters were to become an elite group of demons, fit to kill whomsoever challenged them. We were named the 'Hellstitchers.' We are the reapers of life, for no one truly deserves it."

"Huh... Okay." She paused. "So what happens when you kill someone? Does everyone just see a random guy die out of nowhere? Is there like a pattern for when someone gets killed by one of you?"

"The best Hellstitcher out of the five is granted the title of the Monger," I said, completely ignoring her. "The best of the best! I was powerful enough to claim that rank for my own. My strength is beyond the other Hellstitchers, and my stamina is unmatchable."

"Okay, but... What about my other question?"

"Oh, I think I've answered enough of your questions," I replied.

"You only answered, like, two!"

"That should be good enough. Now give me a name."

"Just one more question? Please?" she begged. "I promise it'll be the last one for now."

"For now?" I said. "Are you planning on asking me more later?"

"Uh, duh!" she exclaimed. "I already told you, I'm interested in your kind! I want to know everything!"

This girl is unbearable. I need to get a name out of her now, before I lose my temper.

"If you would just tell me who to kill, I'll go kill them," I began. "Then I'll answer two more questions. After that, I'm out."

"Are you in a rush or something?" she asked. "Why can't you answer all of them?"

"Because you annoy me. And I'll only answer if you give me the name right now!"

The tight smile she once had completely faded, being replaced by a grumpy frown. She crossed her arms and looked to the side, as if she was pouting. Her attitude was getting her nowhere, and I was ready to strangle her on the fly.

"Fine. I want you to kill Frank Brown. He's my ex."

"Got it," I said, scents plunging into my nostrils.

"He's cheated on me a hundred times," she complained. "With girls that aren't even that good-looking. He deserves it."

I wasn't paying attention. The man she described seemed to live only a few miles away. I could run to the place instead of using my portal, but I couldn't trust this "fan" of mine to leave it alone while I was gone.

"I'll be back," I said before stepping back into my portal. Emilia gave me one last depressed look before dropping her eyes and saying nothing.

***

Arriving in a dark street, dimly lit by the dirty lights lining the road, I focused on the scent Brown was giving off. It was only coming from a few houses away now. Taking a deep breath, I started on my walk.

It was raining in this area. Drops of water continued to pelt my magma-like skin, sizzling with every raindrop. The smell was soothing. It was as if I had found bliss. Though bliss wasn't something a demon would ever have, it was a subject we all dreamed about. This rain was a gateway to a better place.

Striding through the downpour, I reached the house of Frank Brown. It was a duplex, unclear of whose portion was whose. As I got closer to the two doors, I finally noticed a small sign propped up against the porch's wooden railing. It read "Frankie and Emilia."

Scoffing, I promptly phased through the small door. The inside was neatly organized, save for the enormous amount of decorations scattering the floor. It was clearly the owner of Christmas' biggest fan, one with a keen eye for decor. The walls were painted a beautiful green, with red curtains to complement them. The floors were littered with ribbons, ornaments, unhung mistletoe, and bags of candy. Over my stunned silence, I realized there was Christmas music playing in a nearby room. Frank Brown was a nuthead.

Carefully stepping over the mess on the floor, I inched my way to his kitchen, where the horrendous music was blaring with zero remorse. Inside, I found Frank, apron-suited and pimple-riddled. He was mixing a concoction in his man-sized bowl, humming along to the lyrics. Watching him, I leaned up against the wall, spying for any object that seemed to be of high value.

Nothing caught my eye. I walked back out into his living room to see if I could find anything there, but to no avail.

Again, I walked into the kitchen and tried my luck for the second time. Still finding nothing, I searched for another room. His bedroom was my target.

Finding the right room, I switched on the light and got to work. After minutes of opening drawers and exploring nooks and crannies, I eventually came across a framed photo featuring a younger Frank, two children, and two more senior adults. I knew this had to be his family. If he valued Christmas this much in the middle of summer, he had to value his family time a lot more when winter actually came around.

Snatching the photograph, I peeked my head out to the kitchen, making sure I still knew where Frank was. Sure enough, he was still working on his dessert.

After taking one last look at the photo, I caught fire to it and instantly incinerated it. The stench of ash filled the air, and with it, my pure pleasure. But something was wrong. The photo didn't release a screech. I needed to try again.

Frustrated, I shot back into the bedroom to see if there was something else I missed. If I could only stalk this man like I usually did, this job could be done in a matter of seconds.

After what seemed like ages, I abandoned the bedroom, declaring it worthless. Looking through the living room again, I sped up my search but still found nothing. I needed to find another room. If I couldn't uncover something special, I'd have to raze this house until he died.

Exploring a bit more, I found a door to another bedroom, this time undersized and less decorated. It had totes upon totes of what I could only assume to be more Christmas decorations.

Looking around, I found a small shelf displaying actual deco. Among it, there was a small jar, labeled with a quote: "The more you live, the more people come and go. But even after all of them, I'll always stay." I gave a grunt, immediately searching it. This jar carried ash; it was a loved one. Unfortunately, no matter how cherished it could be, no matter how disgusting of a being I was, I was an iconoclast.

Gritting my teeth, I crushed the jar between my palm, letting the ashes pour out over the carpeted floor. Abruptly, from the ashes rose a blackened cloud, followed by a horrifying scream. I won again.

Walking back to the kitchen, I found Frank lying on the floor. He was dead. Smoke was billowing out of his mouth and nose, setting off the duplex's smoke alarm. Cackling at the sight of his death, I headed out of the door and back into the rainy night.

Still laughing, I looked back at the house and pointed at it in a mocking manner.

"Haha! Another victory for me, Frankie!" I shouted. "You pissed off the wrong people!"

I walked away with a fat smile on my ugly face. I splashed through the puddles of water on my way back, messing around while I still could. I arrived at my bloodportal soon after, wishing I could stay and not have to deal with my current problem. I still had no plan. Smile fading, I walked back through my portal.

***

"Hey! Is he dead?" Emilia said, smiling once again.

"Yes, he's dead," I answered. "His innards were incinerated, unfortunately."

"How'd they do that?"

"When a Hellstitcher destroys an item someone loves, it can either do one of two things," I started, clearing my throat. "First, it can set up a chain reaction of events that leads up to their death. Their death is only suited to them; they will die the way they fear the most, within a proper time limit. Second, it can simply burn their guts to a crisp in a matter of less than six seconds. That's only if they don't have the proper time to die the way they fear."

"I didn't know that," she said.

"Yeah...I figured," I said, trying to escape her presence. "Anyway, your soul belongs to the Devil now. Again, when you die, you will be a part of our library. Hope you like it...hot."

I began putting my foot back through my portal when I was stopped by Emilia again.

"Wait!" she snapped. "You still need to answer my questions!"

"Why should I waste my time on you? I've got better things to do."

"It'll only take a minute! Plus, doing this will give you a break between doing these jobs."

"I already get more break time than I need," I argued. "Some of us don't even get a chance to do contracts for weeks."

"Oh, yeah?" she shot back. "If you're really the Monger, so mighty and powerful as you say you are, you can afford to spend another minute away from whatever it is you're pressed with doing!"

I stared into her green eyes with a fiery blaze of anger. If I heard one more lousy sentence coming out of her mouth, I would show her her place!

"You can*not* question my power!" I yelled. "I can do whatever the hell I want, and I don't need some puny human telling me what I can and cannot achieve!"

"Then just prove it! Stay a little bit longer and answer my simple questions," she pleaded.

I growled and plopped on the floor in front of the ritual space. The building shook as I dropped down, and I could feel the floor bending beneath my body.

"Thank you..." she said calmly. "Okay, so...before you were the Monger, were you about just as strong as the other Shadefighters?"

"No. I was stronger," I hissed. "And my powers were superior."

"What powers?"

I lifted an arm up and slowly secreted lava out of the glands wrapping around my forearms. The lava slowly covered my entire arm and dripped onto my legs. The movement was slow but elegant. Nothing could be more beautiful.

"Uhh... Okay," she said, awestruck once again by my abilities. "Um, why can't you just kill someone with your bare hands?"

"It's a devilish trick," I said, still gazing at my lava. "Satan likes to toy with whoever he likes, and he made those rules just to piss us off. If we kill a contract without destroying one of their designated items, we ourselves incinerate. Satan is cruel even to his own children."

"Wow, that's mean."

"Right... But it also exploits the weakness everyone has, being that everyone cares about something."

"Huh. But if you can't complete a contract on time, what happens?"

"Ah... The victim will die anyway, but the

Hellstitcher assigned to the task will get demoted. Satan will turn us into an ordinary demon. No chance of recovering from that."

"Has that happened before?"

"No, but if it does, I'm sure Satan will make a replacement Hellstitcher," I said, my eyes now completely glued to my organic lava. I had to cherish my powers as long as I couldn't come up with a plan soon. How could I live without my lava?

"Okay, okay! Last question: does Satan ever bring you snacks?" Emilia rambled. "I mean, you guys have to get hungry eventually, right? What do you eat?"

I didn't answer. My focus continued to stay on my lava. I wanted to leave and think of something while I still could.

Wait! Something clicked. I knew what I had to do.

"I have to go," I said.

"What? Already? It's just one more question!"

"I wasn't paying attention," I said, stepping back through my portal.

"Wait! Will I get to visit you in Hell?" she yelled one last time.

I gave her a dangerous smile and left her behind. I knew what to do, and I knew exactly when to do it. For now, all I needed to do was wait.

My contract was done.

Chapter Nine

CROOKED

Two days had passed. The doctor was waiting for me. My plan was ready to be sprung into action, as soon as I knew his weapon worked. If the weapon didn't work, I was a dead demon. Tenebris would realize I took him to his death, and he would immediately rat me out. This had to go perfect, for both my sake and the doctor's sake.

Approaching my bloodportal, I paused to take a deep breath. The stench of sweet sulfur ripped the air of Hell. I could feel it course through my blood. I let out a long exhale and continued on my way.

"Only three days left, Decipere," Lucifer spat.

I ignored him, knowing full well either he or I would be dead within three days. Though my time felt limited, it only strengthened my determination. I would claim victory.

***

Coming out of my bloodportal, I landed on the lawn of my target, just as I did last time. The air was dry yet windy. Howling shrieks of wind caressed my ears as I made my way to the house. One step on the porch made me pause again when a unique item caught my attention in the corner of my eye.

A porch swing was swaying slightly in the wind, but the object on it was what got my attention: an embroidered pillow. It looked to be a million years old by now. I turned it around to see a small note stitched onto the corner. It read, "To my beloved son, may our work be fruitful and our lives safe." Surely, this pillow could be used against the doctor, if all else failed. His mother's gift could be the one bluff the doctor had, if he had one at all.

Setting it down, I finally phased through the front door, silently marking my arrival. I walked to the living room to see the doctor was indeed waiting for me, just as expected.

The doctor and I stared at each other for a moment, testing our mettle, before I eventually broke the silence.

"Is it done?" I asked.

"It *is* done," he said, getting off the couch. "Let me show you. My daughter is going to be home soon, so we need to make this brief."

I followed the small man through his bedroom laboratory. On a big desk, with lights hovering above, the weapon stood on a wire rack. It was a glossy white device in the shape of a space-like pistol. Three glass disks rimmed the short barrel, giving it quite the unique design. At the back end of the barrel lay a screen not much larger than a sticky note. The machine was beautiful.

"This is my gizmo!" he proclaimed. "It is a work of art, yet its effects are devastating."

"How does it work?" I asked, still gazing at it. "Does it fire any bullets?"

"No, it fires a beam," he replied, also looking down upon it. "This machine will fire a white beam of light when the trigger is pulled. It needs no reloading at all, but it has limited uses."

"Limited? How limited?"

"Only five shots," he said with a smile. "One for each of your buddies, and eh... Just think of the extra shot as a bit of insurance. In case one misses, or if my current demonic ally feels the need to stab my back."

"Given your circumstance, I'd agree that's justified."

Suspecting me of stabbing his back was an insult I'd never forget. That was the plan all along, but he shall be punished for saying such a thing.

"Yes, it is. Also, there's something I need to let you know. When you bring your other Hellstitchers to me, I must warn you not to let them see me before I fire it."

"I can do that," I replied with a bored expression. "What for?"

"It needs a charge-up in order to fire. It takes six whole seconds to charge and then fires the moment it's done."

"I see a few flaws with your weapon, Doctor," I said snarkily. "With the charging time and the limited shots, why is it only done now?"

"I had to work within my time limits, Decipere," he said with a grumpy tone. "There are a number of reasons why this needs to be done ASAP, and this weapon can do the job in the right hands. My hands *are* the right hands."

"Fine, as long as it works. When shall I bring you the Monger?"

"Tomorrow morning will do. I have the day off work, and I will make sure Lila will already be playing with her friends. Try...nine o'clock?"

"I'll be th—"

I was immediately interrupted by the sound of the front door closing and a little girl's voice following it.

"Daddy, I'm home!" Lila yelled.

The doctor looked at me with wide eyes before running out of the room without so much of a glimpse of hesitation. He started yapping again, but I couldn't make out the words.

Bored, I decided to check the time again. If my suspicions were correct, it'd be exactly six.

I unbuttoned my satchel, pulling out the loosely packaged arm limb, now smelling even worse of decay. Pulling the Rolex off would save space, but carrying an arm around me just felt somewhat humorous.

Six o'clock again. This daughter knew exactly what time to get home and genuinely respected it. That's the first time I'd seen such an obedient child at an already low age. I had to guess she's only eight or nine, but it mattered not. Perhaps it's the love she had for her father that made her so obedient, or maybe she felt bad for him being lonely. Why did it matter? Her father would be dead soon, and she would have to leave everything behind.

I walked out of the room, listening to the family of two ramble on. Everything came into one ear and out of the other. I was silently preparing myself as I strode. Looking back at the doctor, I phased myself out the front door and walked back to Hell.

***

"What's the matter, Decipere? Are you losing your touch?" Satan asked as I returned.

"Sire, I may just need help with this one," I

responded, kneeling down to the fiery throne.

"Ah...so you do?" the Devil said, calmly. "Why don't you ask Tenebris? I just know how much you love spending time with him."

"Pfft!" I mocked. "That mongrel doesn't deserve to work with me!"

"But it will be so!" he roared. "Maybe if you learned to play nice with everyone, I'd give you more Sulfric Growlers to play with!"

"Forget it, I'll figure it out myself," I said, turning away.

"Tick-tock, Decipere." Satan laughed.

I felt my frustration grow as I walked away. Of course, the Devil couldn't know I was bringing Tenebris. I needed only Tenebris himself to know. As wretched a demon he may be, I needed to talk to him just one more time. I would even have to be nice to him just to convince him to join me. His death would satisfy me to no end.

Tomorrow.

Chapter Ten

ARROGANT

The day had come to put Tenebris to rest. Not a one would miss him, and why should anybody? He needed to be put down like a sick dog the day he was created. I walked in utter joy simply thinking about his demise.

As I walked to the coliseum, I spotted Gomorrah crossing the path, likely leaving the ongoing battle. I stuck a finger to him and beckoned him to my place.

As he walked, I noticed a heavy limp coming out of him. He must have gotten his ass handed to him, and maybe it was by exactly who I was looking for.

"Gomorrah," I spoke. "Who hurt you?"

He rushed to me and violently clasped his hands on my shoulders before screaming at the top of his lungs.

"I tried so hard!" he yelled. "I couldn't beat him no matter how c-c-crazy I tried! He too powerful for me! He in arena! Fighting Immolatus now!"

"Who?!" I yelled back, shoving his body off of mine. "Tell me who hurt you, you straightjacket-wearing nuthead!"

"Tenebris! You hate him, right?! Go kill him!"

Gomorrah let out one final cry before attempting to run away, tripping on his own limp in the process.

He lay face down on the ground, groaning but not even trying to get up. He had had enough.

Rolling my eyes, I resumed my walk into the coliseum, pushing demons aside as I made my way to the seats. Sure enough, Tenebris and Immolatus were in the battlefield, duking it out with one another.

Instantly stopping the fight, I called to Tenebris.

"Tenebris! Get your ass over here!" I yelled. "Immolatus, you're finally getting a challenge. I'm ordering fifty demons from the stands to come down and show you who's boss!"

"What?!" Immolatus yelled back. "What's this all about, Decipere?"

I quickly disappeared from the stands, exiting the coliseum while hearing the sounds of demons rise up and screech a battle cry. Not too soon after, Tenebris also came out of the battleground.

"Decipere, what was the point of doing that?" he asked so obliviously.

"Tenebris..." I started, with a long sigh. "I'm working on a contract right now, and I only have two days left to complete it."

"So... Wait, are you asking me for help?"

"Grrr, yes, I am," I growled with hesitation. "I've been too harsh on you, despite your undoubtedly decent work."

Tenebris stared at me for a couple seconds, in shock at what just came out of my mouth.

"I just...need someone's help, all right?" I said. "Being so close to failing this contract made me realize I'm not as great and unstoppable as I once thought."

"But...you said I was unworthy. You said I didn't deserve a name!"

"I did say that, and I was foolish to do so. I was blinded by my own image, captured in chains by my selfishness."

"Right..."

"If you help me, Tenebris, it'll only prove you more capable than I ever thought. Please...forgive me for my past actions. I'll even join you in your contracts, whenever you want it."

A hesitant smile awkwardly made its way onto his face. He laughed for a moment and excitedly started spouting.

"You think I'm a good Hellstitcher! You finally see my worth!" He laughed. "I never thought this day would actually come. It's as if I'm dreaming!"

"Yes, congratulations," I said with a monotone voice.

"Yeah, I'll help you! Why wouldn't I help my hero? Should we let Satan know we're working on this together?"

"No, no," I hastily replied. "This contract needs to be done right now, and we can tell the Devil we worked together once we return. It'll be a nice surprise for him; maybe he'll even slip us a few Sulfric Growlers as a reward."

"Ah, yeah, okay!" Tenebris said excitedly. "Are we going right now, then?"

I turned the opposite way and closed my eyes. Focusing my mind, I slit open a new bloodportal just a few feet in front of me. Turning back to Tenebris, I beckoned him inside.

***

Touching ground on the opposite side of the lawn from my previous bloodportal, Tenebris and I took a deep breath of the cool air, gazing at the doctor's house. Within only a few minutes, it would no longer be just a house anymore; it would become a tomb.

Completely closing the bloodportal behind us, I sealed it shut, making sure nothing could follow us. I turned to Tenebris with a wicked grin before patting him on the back.

"Look at this, we're actually working together," I said.

"Yeah, I've been waiting for this for a long time," Tenebris began. "You have no idea how much it means to me to ask for my help on a contract. It was like, I don't know how, but I finally impressed you enough for you to consider me. You didn't choose Immolatus or Gomorrah, and Atrocify was already working on his own contract, so you chose me."

"Yeah, I did choose you," I said, trying not to sound annoyed. This was entirely unlike Tenebris; I'd never once seen him genuinely happy. It's as if he was hiding behind a façade the entire time I'd known him. Still, I'd never shown the slightest amount of kindness to him in the first place. I felt almost a bit of shame knowing I was leading him to his death.

"So are we gonna destroy some stuff or what?" he asked giddily.

"Hmm...wait out here for a moment. I want you to try and find anything outside this man's house that could kill him. Don't destroy too much, though. The less we destroy, the less of a chance humans will believe Hellstitchers were here."

"His guts could still burn up," he commented.

"Good point," I agreed. "But they may not. If they

do, oh well. But at least if they don't, then Hellstitchers won't be a suitable cause of death."

"You got it, Monger."

I strode up to the porch, looking back once more to see Tenebris wandering around the side of the house. I only needed to keep him occupied for a few moments, just enough to get the doctor ready to shoot him.

I phased myself inside, checking my arm watch at the same time to make sure I arrived on point. I was ten minutes early. It would be fine. I quickly speed-walked my way to the doctor's bedroom, finding him sitting on the side of his bed, playing with his lab coat.

"Ahem!" I announced. "Why the hell are you wearing a lab coat if you're not working today?"

"It makes me feel professional, Decipere," he sassily replied. "Is the Monger here?"

"Yes, he is outside."

"Good," he said, pulling the weapon out of his coat pocket. "Follow me."

We exited the room together, slamming the door closed behind us. The doctor pointed to a spill on the middle of the floor of what looked to be a type of red wine.

"Are you drunk?" I asked with a sarcastic tone.

"Just... I need you to position the Monger right behind that spill," he said, shaking his head. "Make him stand there, so I can get a clear shot without having to aim at a moving target. When he's in position, tap the ceiling three times. I will charge up my gun and blast him as soon as I hear that signal. That also means you'll have to stand closer to the wall so I don't accidentally shoot you instead. Understand?"

"Got it. I'll call him in right now."

I quickly phased through the front door again before searching the front lawn for Tenebris. After seeing nothing, I finally called him.

"Tenebris! Have you found anything yet?"

"Not yet! You were right. This contract is more challenging than most! Besides, there isn't much out here to begin with."

"All right, come to the front door, then."

In a matter of seconds, Tenebris appeared from behind a wall. He looked around before turning his eyes to face mine. I looked at him from atop the porch, disgusted but happily awaiting his demise.

"If there's nothing out here, then we'd best work inside," I said, inviting him to the porch.

"Of course," he stated. "Don't worry, we'll find something. We could even destroy the whole house if it comes to it."

I said nothing, only followed him inside as we phased back into the house yet again. It was time.

The air was silent. My heart began racing faster. Just a few seconds more. This needed to work; it just had to work. The doctor was confident in his abilities, but I was not so sure. I didn't even have a choice in the matter. We walked through the house in silence before getting to the wine spill.

"Hah, hey, Tenebris." I chuckled. "Check this puddle out. It looks like someone got a little too tipsy earlier."

"This guy's a drunk?" Tenebris laughed. "His house is so clean and organized, you'd think he wouldn't be so careless with his booze."

"That's what I thought. Oh, and look at this. If you stand right here, it looks like a big dog with human arms."

I stepped out of the way and to the wall, waiting for him to be in position. In the corner of my eye, I saw the bedroom door was open once again. The doctor was waiting on the other side. I started cracking my knuckles in anticipation. At last, Tenebris would finally die. I hoped.

"Eh, it kind of does," he said, eventually getting into the right position. "But you could also say it looks like an exceptionally tall cat."

I raised my hand to the ceiling. One, two, three knocks.

My heart was beating as fast as it could, and time only seemed to slow down. One second passed at a snail's pace; I only stared at Tenebris with wide eyes. He was still staring at the puddle of wine. Two seconds passed. I dropped my arm to the side, cracking my knuckles again. Three seconds went by. I swallowed my anticipation, letting out an audible gulp. Four seconds. I felt my heart palpitate. Doom was on the horizon. Five seconds passed. Tenebris raised his head to me with confusion. The look on his face would be the last I saw of him. Six seconds.

At last, a bright light erupted, followed by a scream from Tenebris' person. The white beam only lasted for a second before instantly dissipating. Tenebris still stared at me with absolute shock, not knowing what just transpired. There was an enormous gaping hole in his stomach, white veins running along the edge of it. The fire from his horns extinguished, and Tenebris dropped to his knees. With one final gasp of "Decip," he collapsed. Dead.

I let out a gasp of my own, shaking intensively. It worked. The Hellstitcher-killing weapon worked, just as intended.

I turned to face Doc, realizing he was wearing the same face. He turned to me, utterly flabbergasted. He started laughing before rubbing his bald head with his free hand.

"He's dead!" He laughed. "The Monger is dead! We won!"

"Yeah," I said, still putting together what happened.

"Decipere, you must get the others. We have work to do!"

"Hey, Doc, how did you know how to make this weapon?" I asked, ignoring his request. Now that I knew it worked, I had to find out the origin. There could be more like him. I had to eliminate the chance of anyone else killing me.

"Huh? Oh, I had a lot of research to go off on," he started excitedly. "Only other demonic forces can actually kill one of you, so I had to work with a sword I got from another Hellstitcher."

"What?!" I demanded. "How do you have a Hellstitcher's sword? And how do you know this?"

"Listen, the sword is a long story. I snagged it off a Hellstitcher when me and my past workmates were trying to summon one, just to get information. As for knowing what killed you, like I said once before, I have a book. Written by my mother."

"Your mother? But how did she know any of this? This is...unheard of in our world. We've never heard anything about a human obtaining such knowledge, not in the hundreds of years we've lived!"

"Decipere, calm down." He gestured. "I know you didn't think it would work, but like I said, I've been studying Hellstitchers for a long time. Here, I have a gift for you."

He took a step over to me and beckoned for my hand. After opening mine, he dropped a single gold coin into it. I took a look at it; it didn't seem to have any major designs or etchings written on it. It was just a gold coin.

"What's this about?" I asked out of curiosity.

"It's a symbol of allyship," he said, plopping down onto the couch, setting the gun down on the coffee table. "The fact that you kept your word and led one of yours to death meant a lot to me. You'll have to give it back, though. Once we're finally done with this work, you can keep it."

"Okay... But why a gold coin? Why not a new weapon or a decoration for my horns?"

"Do you really want your horns to be decorated?" he asked sternly.

"No, but I can't really do anything with a plain gold coin."

"Right. You're not really supposed to do anything with it, except keep it. It belonged to my mother, and the fact a Hellstitcher helped her in the work she started would make her happy...if she was still alive."

It hit me. His mother was the beginning, and now that she's dead, her son's passing on the work. She had a quest to kill the Hellstitchers, too, but never got far enough. I needed to find the book she made. I needed to know what the doctor knew. Most importantly, I needed to find out who else knew.

"Your mother wrote a book on everything she knew on Hellstitchers?" I asked.

"That's right, she did. Now, I'll need that coin back, if you'd please."

"Wait, how did she even get this knowledge in the first place? She'd have to summon a Hellstit—"

Oh.

"She...probably did," the doctor said with a sigh. "That's the only way *I* see. I never understood why, though. She was a very religious woman. It didn't make any sense."

I stared at the doctor for a moment before glancing at the weapon he placed on the coffee table. I had to take it now and find out the name of his mother.

"Did, eh, anyone else read this book?" I asked, trying to keep my cool.

"Yes..." he said, squinting at me. "Gomez also read it, but he's completely out of the equation now. He wants nothing to do with this work."

He sat up, focusing on my person. We stared each other down for what seemed like hours. He knew what I was about to do, but he's trying to believe I understood the consequences.

"Can I have my coin back, Decipere?" he asked, trying to weed me out of my plans. "You can keep it when we're done. It'll be all yours, and we can each be satisfied with what we've done."

"Hmpf!" I grunted. "No."

Suddenly, I lunged at the weapon, pushing the doctor aside as he attempted to save it. He rolled over the couch in pain and fell to the floor. The weapon was in my hands.

With the time I bought from knocking the doctor over, I unbuttoned my satchel and stored the weapon away. Then, kicking the door to his bedroom open, I partially broke it off its hinges. I came upon the closet holding the safe and this time ripped the entirety of the door off. The safe was still being protected by the holy water, but I had the key on me the whole time.

The doctor rushed in to stop me from grabbing it. I turned my head to see him foaming at the mouth.

"You can't get to it, Hellstitcher!" he yelled. "Don't try it!"

"Hahaha! You underestimate my power!" I shouted back.

With both arms lifted up, I slowly excreted lava out of my veins. In a hypnotizing motion, it soon covered my entire forearms. The doctor gazed at me in confusion before finally realizing what I was doing.

In one fast movement, I plunged my lava-ridden arms into the water and grasped the safe, feeling my lava cool and harden around me. It was now a molten shield, letting me snatch the safe from out of the water and drop it onto the ground. My arms were stiff as rocks, but I got my prize.

"No!" the doctor cried, leaping to the safe.

I kicked and flung the old man to the wall, knocking him out cold. I let a demonic laugh burst out before grabbing the safe again and launching through the wall, into the outside world again.

I had to hide this somewhere safe, where it wouldn't be found by anyone. As long as the doctor couldn't get to it, I'd be perfectly fine.

I started a run into the woods surrounding his house and continued running for a good ten minutes. I knew he'd assume I took the switch, but I didn't need it. I couldn't risk accidentally activating it while carrying the weapon around. What could be the use of keeping it anyway?

After a solid extra five minutes of running, I finally set the safe down and moved it into the brush surrounding a pair of large trees. It'd be comfortable here, as long as no one came looking for it. My weapon was safe.

Sitting down, I debated on what my next plan of action should be. I needed to force the doctor to make a weapon capable of killing Satan. I would have him stay up all night and day if I had to. There wasn't enough time to give him a break. But then again, I needed to find his dead mother in Hell and get some information out of her.

I groaned, knowing full well there's little hope for me. The Devil would notice Tenebris was gone, and when he did, he'd naturally suspect me as the culprit of the disappearance. Immolatus knew I was with Tenebris, too. I needed to kill Immolatus before he slipped the lip, if he hadn't already. That's just another risk I had to take. If the doctor couldn't make another weapon in time as well, I'd have to find some way to kill him, just to keep myself from being demoted. I could not be demoted.

I hopped up to my feet, knowing where to go next. I didn't even know the mother's name, but I sure as hell knew how to find it.

***

Arriving at my destination, I closed my portal

behind me. I felt the rough texture of the parking lot under my toes. The sun beat down particularly hard today, yet I didn't feel an ounce of discomfort. Taking a look at the building in front of me, I confirmed it was the right place to be: Sol's Technologies.

Waiting outside for an eternity, I watched as people came and went about. I considered taking a nap to pass time, but I had to make sure no one incidentally bumped into me.

I continuously gazed at my watch while waiting, resting until it reached four thirty. That was closing time.

When the time came, floods of people strode out of the front door. All wearing lab coats and suits, they quickly dispersed from the area, letting me safely head inside.

All around was still lit up, as some employees were still packing up their things. Some scientists were still running experiments. The building felt even bigger than I remembered, but I still knew my way to the doctor's laboratory.

Phasing inside, I noticed there was still a lone worker here. He was writing something on a series of sticky notes, but I didn't bother to observe.

I sat down on my knees in front of a computer. It was the same one my target used when I stalked him. I pressed a few buttons and realized I had no idea how to operate one of these things. I tried for multiple minutes pressing various buttons to try and get the computer to turn on, but no luck.

I took another glance at the lone worker, seeing he was still writing on those sticky notes. Standing back up, I opened my satchel to grab my last Sulfric

Growler. This one was going to count.

Crushing the Sulfric Growler between my fingers, I stuck it under the scientist's nose, allowing him to smell the horrendous aroma. He gagged for a moment before coughing repeatedly. He kept his focus maintained at his sticky notes, not even bothering to look around and determine where the smell was coming from.

"The hell was that?" he said under his breath.

"That was me!" I yelled, catching his attention.

"Shit!" he screamed, falling to the ground. I laughed at his clumsiness, pointing a finger while doing so.

He bolted to the door, but I was quicker. Blocking his path with my colossal body, I pushed him to the ground again.

"What are you? What are you gonna do to me? Someone help! Please!" he screamed.

"Shut up!" I howled.

"Help! Please!" he continued screaming. "There's a monster in here! He's trying to kill me!"

"I said shut up!" I yelled again. "I'm not going to kill you! Now just sit down and listen!"

The scientist did no such thing. He scrambled to his feet and started running in the other direction, stopping in the corner, standing directly across the big table in the middle.

"Please don't hurt me! I've done nothing bad in my life! I don't deserve this! Someone help!"

Angrily, I phased through the giant table to stand directly in front of him, giving him nowhere to go. I grabbed both of his arms as he tried to squirm out, but I held tight and pushed him against the wall.

"Calm. Down!" I yelled one final time. "I am not here to hurt you. I need you to access a computer for me!"

"And you're not gonna kill me afterward? I don't believe that! You're a demon, aren't you? All you want is for people to die!"

"No, I—" I growled. "You don't have a choice! Either you help me, or I'll kill you, and I'll find someone else to do it, and then I'll kill them!"

I couldn't get someone else to help me even if I tried, but this man needed to believe me.

"Yo—you're not gonna kill me if I work the computer for you, though?" he stuttered, tears beginning to stream out of his eyes.

"That's right. And you'll never see me again afterward, you got it? You can continue on with your worthless life, and you won't ever have to see me again."

"Uh, yeah!" He nodded nervously. "I can do that."

"Good," I said. "Now turn the computer on, and get me some information."

"Okay, okay, okay, okay," he said, shakily approaching the computer. He tried pressing a button, but nothing happened. He crouched down below the desk and plugged in some sort of cable.

"It, uh, wasn't plugged in." He hesitated. "But I can work it now."

"Good, now I need you to get all the information you can on one person. Most importantly, I need to get his mother's name."

"Y-yeah, sure..." he said, continuing avoiding eye contact. "Just give me the guy's name?"

"Of course."

***

"Is, uh, is this the guy you're looking for?" the scientist asked.

"Yes, that's him. Now get out of the way, and let me read!"

I scrolled through the paragraphs of information on the doctor. I found his age, date of birth, and height. But no mother. I continued scrolling down to find an article titled "Familial Ties." Bingo.

His mother's name was Monica. I knew how to get to her now. The Library of Souls was my next destination, but time was limited. If I could reach it without the Devil knowing, I could return back to Earth with time to get a new weapon from the doctor.

"Your job is done," I told the scientist. "What's your name, maggot?"

"Um, my name..." he began, playing with his fingers. "My name's Dave. I work here with your guy. He and I develop—"

"All right, that's enough, Dave. I don't actually care. Now, begone!"

He wiped the tears from his eyes before sprinting out of the lab. What a cowardly baby he was. I should've picked someone who looked even a little tougher. They could've done the same thing from a different lab.

It didn't matter anymore. I needed to get back to Hell and into the library. Finding out who else knew about the Hellstitchers was priority number one.

Chapter Eleven

I woke up dazed and confused. I had forgotten what transpired before I got knocked out. My glasses were lying on the floor next to me with one of the lenses popped out. I slowly sat up and held the broken glasses in my hands. Getting my dirty fingerprints all over, I inserted the lens back into the frame and took a glasses cleaner out of my lab coat pocket.

After cleaning them up, I put them back on and looked at the world around me. There was a gaping hole in the wall. The window was completely shattered, and bits of wood and stone lay scattered just outside.

Decipere! That vile thief! My weapon was now gone, and with it my fail-safe. I had assumed it was protected with the utmost security, but Decipere had exactly the right tools to get past it. How could I be this unlucky?

I struggled to get to my feet, now feeling an injury present in my leg. Limping my way out, I almost tripped on the dead Hellstitcher still lying on my floor. I sat at my dining table and put my head in my hands. I had failed. One Hellstitcher may be dead, but another one took my only means of destroying them. I'd lost.

No, it was not over. Decipere must come back at some point. Without killing me, he faced death himself. That could be my opportunity to get my gun back. When Decipere was dead, I could retrieve my weapon and get back to work. I'd need someone to do the ritual again, and multiple times. Gomez wouldn't do it... But maybe I could hire someone willing.

Gomez. I had to tell him what happened. He'd be quite disappointed, but I must keep him in the loop. Searching for my cell phone within my coat, I realized I had lost that, too. Getting up from my seat, I began a search.

I checked the living room and kitchen first, with no luck. My garage was third, but nothing came out of it. I began to have a suspicion it was in my bedroom, getting lost when I was knocked into the wall. Checking there, I looked all over. Finding it under my bed, I noticed a pair of glowing eyes from the darkness. I quickly snatched my cell phone before lifting the bed up, revealing the critter hiding underneath.

A raccoon, the chunkiest I'd ever seen, shot out from under the bed in a scurry. He ran out of the gaping hole in the wall, making it clear I had to cover it up ASAP. Before that, however, I had to call Gomez.

Before doing so, I realized I needed to get rid of the body in my house. The Hellstitcher's carcass was huge; I had no idea how I was going to dispose of it. I grappled onto its hand and first attempted to drag it along the floor. I planned to take it to the hole in my wall and set it down just outside in the woods.

After getting only a few inches dragging it, I decided to turn the body so I could roll it. Several minutes passed by before I got it into the prime position. Giving my best strength, I pushed and rolled the body into my bedroom. The horns proved to be an issue, getting stuck on the doorframe, but with enough effort, I was able to dislocate its head and bring it all the way through.

Finally dragging him out, I lay his body down in a slumped position just outside the wall. When the rest of the Hellstitchers were dead, I could bring their bodies out here and donate them to science. My work would go beyond what my mother's vision entailed, and maybe I'd even be able to afford a decent retirement.

Heading back inside, I took a rest sitting down on the couch. Switching my phone on, I hit the call button and dialed Gomez. It rang multiple times before I finally got him to pick up.

"Hello?" Gomez asked.

"Hey, buddy." I spoke in a croaky tone. "Ahem. How are you holding up?"

"Uh, hey, man," Gomez said back. He did not sound to be in a talkative mood. "I'm...pretty fine. I'm in Utah right now, visiting Salt Lake, so it's all going fine on my end. What's up?"

"Um..." I struggled. "That's great, Gomez. You're not really going to like what you hear, though."

"Oh, no." He sighed. "Please, please, please, please don't tell me it has anything to do with the Hellstitchers."

"I'm sorry to disappoint."

"Gah! What happened? Are you okay? Are you hurt, or safe? Is Lila safe?"

"Please, just one question at a time, all right?" I said, putting my feet up on the coffee table. "Me and Lila are safe, but I think my leg was sprained. I had a situation with a Hellstitcher."

"Are you going to the doctor's?" he asked.

"I *am* a doctor. I'll be fine," I said with ease. "I'm not just an expert in technology, you know. I have multiple years of being a medical doctor."

"All right, then what happened?"

"I, erm, tried to work with the Hellstitcher assigned to me."

"Why would you do that?"

"He refused to hand over the other Hellstitchers unless I agreed to let him live. I didn't have any problems with it, as long as I was still able to kill him after the rest."

"So did he know you were planning to double-cross him?" he asked curiously.

"I don't believe he did. He only seemed interested in having the weapon," I said. I knew he was going to betray me eventually, but I didn't think it would be this early in the mission. Double-crossing him would have kept me and Lila safe and secured the world's future.

"Oh no..." Gomez whined. "He took the weapon, didn't he?"

I could hear the utter disappointment in his voice. He was distraught. I had to tell him, but he may just be saved.

"Yeah," I replied quietly. "He took it after seeing that it worked, and he took off."

"It worked?" he asked. "So you got at least one of them?"

"Yes, I did. Only a minute after killing it, though, the Hellstitcher made off with both the weapon and the failsafe."

"How in the world was he able to get to that thing? It was protected by every measure you could've taken."

The conversation narrowed as I told him the rest of the events. I told him about Decipere's powers and how he should come back. Gomez wasn't too thrilled about the situation as a whole, nor was I. We discussed a game plan, but I told him I was exhausted. The talk didn't last too long, but all I wanted to do was rest and think of my next move alone.

I was unsure of what would happen next. After Decipere was dead, I'd need to invest the rest of my retirement for a new weapon. That's only if I didn't get mine back, but it's a valid possibility. The remaining time I had had to be dedicated to this work. I wouldn't allow it any other way.

My thoughts ran on and on. I considered Lila taking over my work if I had passed away beforehand, but I didn't know if I wanted her dealing with all the trouble it entailed. I could get her blueprints and instructions on how to build the gun, and I could leave behind all of my fortune to pay for it. Lastly, I could update my mother's book with my findings and have her keep it safe. I didn't want my little girl to be put in this kind of danger, so it'd have to be the very last option.

Suddenly hearing the door open, I jumped to my feet and rushed to see who it was. It was Lila, looking gleeful as always.

"Hey, Munchkin!" I said with a new smile.

"Hi, Daddy!" she yelled, running for a hug. I embraced her around me and picked her up.

"Is it already six?" I asked. "Didn't feel like you were gone for that long."

"No, it's like, uh, one, I think," she said hesitantly. "You lost the time?"

"Yeah, Daddy took a quick nap," I said, lowering her to the ground. "Why are you back so soon?"

"I forgot my snacks in the fridge. I love eating snacks with my friends."

"I know you do, Munchkin," I said. "That's why I ate them all!"

"Noooo, you didn't!" she said, laughing.

"Mmm, but I could have. I was so tempted to just gobble them up myself."

"Nuh-uh, you would never do that!" she said, running to the refrigerator. "My daddy would never do that!"

"I'd like to see if that's true!" I said, opening a cupboard. I got out a plate and started gathering food of my own.

"Uh, Daddy?" Lila asked innocently.

"What's up?"

"I, um, wanted to know why there was a hole in the wall."

"Oh," I paused, "well, um...I'm trying to find a weak spot in the walls. I found one in my room, so I got a crew to bust a big hole in it."

"A crew?" she asked, putting her snacks in her backpack.

"Yeah, a crew," I said, trying not to act conspicuous. "They're coming back later to rebuild it. It could be tonight or tomorrow. I don't know yet."

"If you want it done today, I can help you, Daddy."

"Aw, you know I love your help," I said, poking her nose. "But I'd rather have you play with your friends. You still have a few years before you can help with construction."

"No-o-o-o, I'm old enough."

"Nine-year-olds are not old enough. Sorry, Lila. No matter how cute you are."

"When can I be old enough?" she asked excitedly.

"Hm, let me think about that. I'll give you an answer once you get back, all right?"

"Okay, Daddy!"

She jumped up to hug me tight. I pulled her close and let go. She took off again, out the door.

"Bye, Daddy!" she yelled, closing the door behind her.

I sighed and looked around. Eyes relaxing on my new sandwich, I took it to the table and began to eat. If only Lila knew what was going on. If only she was old enough, so I could tell her. She's just a child; she wouldn't be able to handle knowing any of this. Still, it'd be a lot easier if she did.

It was a mistake agreeing to a Hellstitcher's wishes. Decipere was a demon and a deceiver; I should have known better than to trust him for a second, but I didn't have any way of knowing whether what he was saying was true or not. I couldn't risk calling his bluff, and I had to get the Monger first. I had no doubts Decipere was the real Monger all along. I should have killed him as soon as I killed the other one, but it's too late. All I could do right now was wait for him to rear his ugly head again.

I sat back after finishing my meal and closed my eyes. All I could do was wait. Wait and prepare.

Chapter Twelve

UNLOYAL

After landing back into Hell, I began running to the library. I needed to get answers as fast as I could. If Monica was really in there, she'd have to tell me everything. If the Devil found out what I was up to, this may well be the last time I could be in Hell without a target on my back.

Swiftly, I bolted to the entrance without a moment to spare. Only a few seconds away—I could make it!

Suddenly, my body came to a screeching halt. Satan had appeared directly in front of me, in his more miniature status. His lava was flowing particularly fast. His expressions were as deadly as a viper.

"My lord!" I yelped. "How may I help you?"

"You can help me by finishing your contract!" he yelled. "How is it that you only have one more day to complete it?! The last time this happened, you were schlubbing around Hell the entire time, but no, you are actively working on this one, yet it's not done!"

"Sire, I can explain myself," I pled, hiding my own anger.

"Let's take a walk, Decipere," he ordered. "Follow me."

He grabbed my arm, yanking it alongside him. I

tried desperately to break free of his grasp, but he was much more powerful than me. He was the only one able to do this, and for that, I must kill him.

"Decipere, I cannot let you into the library until you've done your task," he started, "but I need to know why you haven't completed it yet."

"Lucifer, I feel my target is lacking an item to kill him with," I said, gritting my teeth. "I am trying to connect with his deceased relatives in hopes of finding some information."

"That almost sounds believable. But it's not as believable as what I think is really going on."

"And what's that?"

"My top worker, my Monger, is lazing off yet again! You are shirking your duties to go and play around in the library when you only have a day left to complete the contract! And to add on top of that, while working on the contract for four days, you've gotten nowhere, which leads me to believe you're not even making an attempt at it!"

"You are outrageous!" I shouted.

"Am I, Decipere?" he argued. "Then what's really going on here?"

"I told you! There's nothing else!"

"That's the wrong answer, Monger."

"No, it is not! I told you exactly why I was running to the library!" I yelled again.

"If that's your final answer, you are dead! Do you hear me? Dead!"

Silence flooded the air around us. I was shocked at this threat against my very life. The Devil had never been serious about this before, but I knew he meant it this time. I had to tell him something else, but I couldn't think of anything that he wouldn't dub bullshit.

"My contract can see me," I said.

"You're lying; that's not possible." He started back.

"He can talk to me, see me, and threaten me."

This caught his attention.

"Threaten you how?" he asked curiously.

"He claims to be making a weapon that can kill a Hellstitcher," I continued. "Judging by the fact that he knows how to communicate with me, I have a feeling his weapon is a legitimate danger."

"Is this a sorry excuse to miss the contract? To make something up to get you out of trouble?"

"No!" I backfired. "He said he had a mother, one that summoned a Hellstitcher before. She got information from him and passed her knowledge onto my target. I was being set up to be slaughtered."

"Ah... And you were going to the library to see what she knew, then?"

He believed me. And he knew. Given the time I had left, I felt it didn't make a difference that he knew now. I would've had to kill him or die in a day anyway.

"Yeah." I sighed. "I haven't found anything to kill him with, either. He's been preparing."

"Go to the library, then," Satan demanded. "When you're done, meet me at the throne and tell me what she knows. I still have work to do up there."

"Understood," I said, treading away.

"Wait, Decipere!" he called. "If you don't come back from the library, you're dead!"

I shook my head and continued on my way. I heard Satan laughing behind me. I had to play his game for now, but it wouldn't matter in the end. It would be him who was dead, and I would be the dictator of Hell! The other three Hellstitchers would have no choice but to submit.

Getting back to the Library of the Damned, I quickly made my way inside. Standing upon her perch, the Silent Librarian awaited me. She was feasting on a raw piece of unidentifiable meat. Clearing my throat, I interrupted her meal.

"Librarian, I need to see someone special today."

She said nothing, as per usual, but leaped down from her perch and stuck her gray hand out for an offering. I had one gift left. I opened my satchel up and slipped my Rolex watch off of the arm. Kissing the limb goodbye, I placed it in the Librarian's hand. She stared at it for a moment and jumped back in her perch, laying it down on the already-full plate of meat.

After jumping back down, she beckoned me inside the gate and into the full library. Stopping at a rotted book, she opened it up and shoved it into my giant yellow hands. I spent nearly a minute searching for Monica's full name. When I finally found it, I gave the book back to the Librarian, pointing at my target.
***

After only a few minutes of wandering around the Sanguine River, the Librarian finally stopped. With one graceful movement, she threw her hands into the sky and plunged them into the river. I stood and watched her go to work. It was simply majestic. I had seen very little of this action; it's not every year that we needed to fish out someone in specific.

Suddenly, the Librarian caught someone. Pulling them out, it was revealed to be the woman I was looking for. Perfect.

She threw Monica down on the floor before wiping the blood on her dark robes. Monica was screaming the whole time, clawing at her curly gray hair. Before leaving, the Librarian gave me one final nod and walked away.

Monica's screams turned into crying, with the woman only barely lifting herself off the ground. I quickly grabbed her by the head and turned it to face mine.

"Monica! Do you know who I am?" I yelled, raising my voice above her cries.

"No, I don't know you!" she yelled.

"Well, get comfy!" I shouted back. "You're about to know me very well."

"What do you want with me? I didn't do anything!"

"You did quite a lot, Monica. You did so much that you guaranteed a place for yourself in Hell!"

"I didn't want to... I couldn't help myself!" she cried.

"Tell me! Why did you summon a Hellstitcher?"

"W-What?" she said, slowing her cries down. "How do you know that?"

"Your prince of a son let me in on that," I said sternly. "And to add on to that, he tells me he got all of his knowledge on Hellstitchers from you."

"Why did he tell you that?" she asked. "He is supposed to kill you monsters, not strike up a conversation."

"I simply offered him help. I proved to be valuable to his operation, and I got him to spill a bit. I'm sure he didn't think I'd be able to reach you. I'm sure he didn't think I could use that information against him. He had all the cards, demanding the Monger to be brought before him. But I am a loyal Hellstitcher. I would rather die than lead one of my own to their death. He had no choice but to accept my conditions, and as I helped him, I learned about you and your book."

"The book should already be destroyed by now!" she yelled. "You'll never get to it!"

I growled in anger before throwing a kick to her side, launching her over the river. She gurgled in pain, grasping her stomach as she tried to get up again. I leaped across the river to join her and snatched her by the throat.

"Then *you'll* have to tell me!" I demanded. "Tell me what you know about the Hellstitchers! Tell me who else knows!"

"Try harder, demon," she whispered. "My son is going to kill you and your grotesque group of Hellstitchers. How many has he killed already? Two? Three? Maybe four?"

"I don't have to answer a single question that comes out of your mouth," I whispered back. "I will ask, and you will answer."

I dropped her to the floor, pummeling her into the ground with a single fist. She continued to cry out, begging me to stop.

"Answer me, lady!" I yelled.

"Stop, stop! I'm not telling you anything, no matter how hard you hit me!"

"You'll experience the worst beatings of your eternal life in Hell, every day after now. I will come back, and I will fish you out and bruise you until my hands hurt!"

This was not true. I had no intention of returning to her, but I needed her to talk. She'd open up one way or another.

"I don't care! You won't be alive to do it! My son will kill you, and you aren't stopping him!"

"Gahh!" I yelled in frustration. "All right, then, Monica! How about I make a deal with you instead?"

"I'm not making another deal with a demon. Whatever you're about to suggest, forget it!"

"Is that right? You're a believer in God, aren't you?"

"Yes, I am. It's a shame I had to end up in Hell, but knowing you Hellstitchers would all die, it was worth it."

"Whatever, lady, just listen to me."

She went silent but looked away to avoid my glaring eyes. I knew she'd accept my "offer;" it's too tempting for her.

"If you tell me what you know, Monica," I offered, "I'll erase your name from the library. It'll set your soul free, and your eternal life could be in Heaven."

She turned back to me with wide eyes. Still silent, she thought for a moment. Her eyes then turned into a glare.

"I won't fall for this," she said angrily. "You are a deceiver. It's in your nature, as a demon."

"You *will* accept my offer, or your son is dead!" I yelled.

"Sure he is. If he's managed to scare you into seeking me out, I know you can't kill him. He's already won."

The old lady started laughing at my defeat, but I still had one more option.

"No, he hasn't," I said calmly.

"Oh, yes, he has!" She laughed. "And I'm so proud of him!"

"I'm going to kill him with my bare hands," I said without hesitation.

"And what? Get yourself killed? Tell your jokes to another fallen soul."

I got up close to her, setting my disgusting face only inches away from hers. I glared at her with fiery eyes and started huffing smoke out of my nostrils.

"I mean it. Your son is dead!" I yelled. "I am not going to let him finish off my race, my brothers!"

"You wouldn't dare," she said back, her tone serious.

"I would!" I lied. "I already told you once, I would rather die than lead my kin into their demise!"

Her eyes widened again. I could see the panic stretched out across her face.

"You can't!" she pleaded. "Y-You have to be bluffing! I know you won't do that!"

"Ohhh," I laughed back, "so you want to test it out, is that right?"

"No, no, no, no!"

"Tell me then, lady."

She started crying again, burying her head in her ghostly white legs. She wailed for ages, knowing she lost. I stood at her feet, waiting for her to be done. I didn't even have an hour to be here, so she needed to spit it out pronto.

"Get a grip, Monica," I said. "Tell me, who else knows what you know? And why did you summon a

Hellstitcher?"

"No one knows!" she bawled. "It's only me and my son! I left the book for him when I got hospitalized for the last time! I knew my end was close, and I couldn't complete my work, so I had to pass it onto him! I told him not to bring anyone else into the situation!"

"Why'd you tell him that?" I asked again.

"Because no one would believe him. The vast majority of the world already doesn't know what a Hellstitcher is, and I was afraid he would lose trusted ones if he tried to get them to help. I fear his wife has already left him because of it."

"That man doesn't have a wife. She's dead."

"What?! So it's just him? Is he all alone?"

"No, no," I said hastily. "He has a young daughter. She's about eight or nine. They seem to have a beautiful relationship. You already know how tragic it would be if that girl was left all alone, with no father to love her anymore."

"You can't kill him! You can't!" she screamed, getting to her feet.

"He's not going to die!" I lied. "Unless you decide it's best to withhold more information from me!"

"No, no, I won't! What was your other question?"

"Why did you summon a Hellstitcher?" I asked. "It doesn't make sense to sell your soul to the Devil just so you can kill his reapers one day. It's especially strange for a Christian to do it."

"I... That's very personal."

"I don't care if it's personal. You will answer it," I demanded again.

"Uhm... Okay, Hellstitcher. It's not a short story, just a warning."

"Then make it quick," I said, sitting down on the heated rock floor.

"Fine."

Chapter Thirteen

My name was Monica Black. Black was my maiden name; I had to use it in public so I didn't get associated with my husband. When I married him, he was a thoughtful and caring man. He was sweet, charming, and so very loving. As perfect as he was, he became a different man altogether after we married.

We met in a church, after I moved across states. It was my first time at this church, and he offered me a seat next to him. After the session ended, he introduced himself. Mark was such a simple name, and I'd never met a Mark before. What a vile man he'd become.

The day I lost it was ten years after the marriage. Mark wanted kids, but I had never wanted kids. Day after day we fought about it, and eventually the sparks turned into a wildfire.

***

"Monica," Mark said, "do you see all the kids playing in the park on your way to work?"

"Yes, why?" I asked.

"Don't you wish you could have a child of your own to join them?" he said, staring out the window. "Or even children? They would have so much fun."

"I've already..." I said with a sigh. "Mark, how

long is it going to take you to realize we aren't having kids?"

We just got home from church. I wanted to unwind and make some arts and crafts, as I usually did on a Sunday afternoon. Mark wanted to fight about children. Again.

"I'm not accepting that, Monica," he spat. "One day we're going to have kids, whether you like it or not."

"We established at the beginning of our relationship that we aren't having kids. I told you the day after we met that I never wanted kids."

"That's gonna have to change."

"No, it doesn't. Why are we arguing about this every single day? If you really want kids, you're not going to have them with me."

He shot up, fists clenched on both sides. He got angry faster than he could force a smile. I was never afraid of him, though. He'd never tried to hurt me in his anger, no matter how irritated he'd gotten.

"Yes, I will!" he said, raising his voice. "You're the one I love, who I want to be with, and you love me! And if I want children, I'm going to have them with you!"

"You are not going to have a child with me. I'm getting my tubes tied next month, just so I can make sure of that."

This baffled him. His face grew pale, and his rage turned into sorrow.

"You what?" he said, astonished. "But our family line, i-it's important to keep up."

"Mark, it's not our family's choice whether the line continues on or not. I don't want kids, and I never will want kids. Nobody can just force me to change my mind."

"I will!" he yelled again, getting closer. "My lineage will not die with me! Do you hear me?"

"I hear you, but it won't happen! I'm telling you, I don't want kids!"

"Urgh!" he growled, clawing at his head before pointing at me. "You will do what I say, and I will not hear any arguing!"

"Mark..." I began softly. "I'm not your slave. We're married because we love each other, and we agreed to be partners in life."

"Clearly, you don't love me as much as you say. Otherwise we'd be discussing what names we want our kids to have!"

"I do love you! And you're breaking my heart!" I cried.

"You're a liar!" he yelled, pushing me against the wall. "We are going to have kids, whether you love me or not! We are going to be a big, happy family, and I'm done negotiating about it!"

"Stop, get off of me!" I shouted back, trying desperately to throw him off. He was much stronger than I was; it was an unfair advantage.

Suddenly, he grabbed me by the shirt and threw me onto the ground, knocking the wind out of me. I didn't have any time to react to the hand coming at my face. My cheek burned, and tears started to form in my eyes. My husband had lost it, and he's taking out his anger on me.

"If you won't submit with words, then I'll have to force the submission out of you," he said, taking off his shirt.

"What are you doing?" I asked, trying to hide my tears.

"I'm doing what needs to be done," he said. "That's all."

He began unbuckling his belt, and that's when I realized what was about to happen. I quickly brought myself to my feet before feeling the whip of his belt across my back. I knelt down in pain, trying not to make any resemblance of a sound. I looked back to see he was completely naked, save for the socks he still had on.

"No, no, no, please get away from me," I begged, tears streaming from my eyes. "Please just let me go! I'll let you adopt a kid, I promise!"

"I don't want to adopt some random child!" he roared. "It has to be my blood, mine! Mine and yours!"

I made a run for it, bolting for the back door. I was only inches away before I felt a snag on the collar of my shirt, instantly yanking me away from it. Mark gripped the back of my neck and forced me to the wall again. I fought hard to pull the hand off me, but I felt a punch cracking in on my cranium. I felt dizzy, like I was seconds away from passing out.

Mark yanked me by my brunette hair, holding me close, and started tearing my shirt off of my body. Weak in my arms, I attempted to claw at his neck to get him off of my shirt, but he didn't let up. He tore it off and, without hesitation, went for my jeans next.

I started crying for help, screaming at the top of my lungs. Mark only went faster, pulling my pants down at the speed of light. He threw me to the floor once again, landing on my stomach this time. I tried to get up as soon as I hit the ground, but I felt the body weight of Mark pressing me down. I felt another whip from his belt, more violent than the last. I writhed in pain as he continued whipping me until blood shot out. My bare back was utterly destroyed. I continued crying out, hoping someone would hear my call, but no one ever came.

"Monica, I'm sorry I had to do this," Mark finally said, breathing heavily. "But you gave me no choice."

I only cried. My husband of ten years turned on me and beat me to a pulp. I loved him so much; why did he have to do this? I thought we would be happy together, just being the two of us. With no kids in the equation, we'd only have ourselves to give time to. That's what we agreed to.

"Be a good girl, and stay quiet, all right?" Mark said, getting on top of me.

"No! Help! Help me!" I screamed.

He swiftly threw a punch to the back of my head, knocking it down again. He followed it up by grabbing my mouth, keeping it from screaming again. I was dizzy; my vision was blurry. I could barely focus on what happened next. I felt him rip the rest of my clothes off and go to work. It was painful, but I couldn't fight back. He kept it going for what seemed like hours, not giving any breaks whatsoever. He didn't seem to be slowing down, either. I tried shaking his hand off my mouth multiple times, but his grip only got tighter. Eventually he started choking me. I could only groan in pain. In a matter of seconds, my thoughts left me, and my vision went dark.

***

It'd been four months since the first incident. Every day afterward, he continued to have his way with me, just to make sure I would get pregnant. I tried to escape the house, but he went as far as threatening to murder my parents just to keep me home. I didn't want to find out if he was being serious about it, so I stayed put. He cut the cords to the phones, too, to keep me from communicating with anyone. All I could ever do was sit at home and wait for him to force me down on the ground again. The amount of measures he went to to keep me from getting away were immaculate. There was no way out.

Today two of our friends from church visited us, and Mark had me put makeup on to hide my bruises. I wanted to tell them what he was doing to me, but he watched me like a hawk. I wasn't able to gain even a second alone with our visitors.

And then it happened. Mark agreed to go out with them, leaving me all alone at the house. He took both car keys with him and gave me a warning as he left. It was my only chance.

Only minutes after he took off, I donned my shoes and socks and washed all the makeup off. I took off out of the house and ran directly to my best friend's house. Her name was Cherry, and she lived only five blocks away.

I knocked on her door as fast as humanly possible. Knocks turned into banging, until Cherry eventually swung the door open.

"Monica, why are you banging on my door so hard? And why haven't I seen you in months? I keep trying to stop by and send letters, but I've gotten nothing. Is Mark being protective again?"

"No, Cherry, I need your help," I begged. "I need to come inside."

"Sure, of course!"

I stepped inside and threw my arms around her in no time. She laughed and hugged me back before finally realizing I was in trouble.

"Hey, honey are you okay?" she asked.

I stopped hugging her, bringing my face into the light.

"Oh, shit!" She gasped. "Who did this to you?"

"It was Mark!" I cried. "He beat me. We got into an argument about kids again, and he beat me! He forced me to the ground, and he...HE RAPED ME! I never wanted to have a kid, but he raped me for weeks on end! I'm pregnant now, and I can't do anything to stop him from doing it anymore!"

I collapsed in Cherry's arms, hugging her as tight as I could. I needed to stay away from Mark, but I didn't have enough time to keep him away from my parents.

"I kept telling him that I didn't want kids, and he just decided that I didn't have a choice!" I cried again, lifting my face up. "I need your help, Cherry. Look what he did to my back!"

I turned around and lifted up my shirt, showing the abhorrent markings the belt made on my flesh. Cherry gasped again, and tears began to fall from her eyes as well.

She rushed me and hugged me tighter than I could hug her. She started crying with me, and we wept together, just trying to get it all out.

"We...are going to make him pay, all right?" Cherry said, holding my face up to hers. "Follow me into the bedroom. I know how to deal with this."

"I don't want to call the cops! I need him dead!" I

exclaimed. "So he can't hurt anyone else! Please, Cherry, I don't know how we're supposed to deal with this."

"Mon..." she started. "I understand, and I agree. We can make that happen, all right? Just be open-minded about this solution. You're not going to like it a single bit."

"If you're suggesting I murder him myself, I can't! I can't kill someone, I just can't! Even if it's a monster like Mark..."

"You won't have to kill him yourself. I'll explain what's going to happen while I set it up, you got that?"

I nodded my head softly, looking to the floor all the while. I walked behind her, sniffling. I had no idea what she had planned, but it needed to take care of Mark as soon as possible. I needed to be safe, but I was risking my parents' lives by escaping Mark's clutches.

Cherry dug through a pile of totes and pulled the only red tote out of her closet. She threw the lid open and quickly dumped out the contents. An entire snake corpse fell out, along with a small jar of blood and multiple candles.

She quickly opened the jar and started spilling the blood on the floor, forming it into a giant circle.

"Look, Monica, do you know what a Hellstitcher is?" she asked.

"No...what is that?"

"A Hellstitcher is an agent of Satan, born to kill. They can murder anyone you want, for the price of your soul."

"What?! I'm not making a deal with the Devil!" I said in shock. "I am a child of God. I would never betray him."

"Monica, if you really want him dead, this is your only option. You already said you can't kill him yourself, and I doubt you have the money to hire some sort of hitman."

"Yeah, I can't kill him because murder is a sin. It's in the Ten Commandments. That, and I probably wouldn't have the guts to do it anyway."

"Would you rather him be in prison?" she suggested, now forming a star within the circle. "Or even have the jury take too long to decide whether he's actually guilty or not?"

"There's enough evidence on my back, but..." I thought about it more. If I really had to sell my soul just to get Mark dead, I may as well try and learn about the Hellstitchers themselves. I could even find a way to kill them if I was determined enough. The world couldn't have such vile beasts.

"Okay...let's do it," I said firmly.

"Good, now just let me finish making the outline," she said, finishing up the pentagram. She lit up her five candles and placed them at the five points of the star. The floor would need a heavy cleaning after we're done here.

Cherry handed me the dead snake, plopping it on my shoulder. I sat down in front of the pentagram and held the snake to my eyes.

"What do I do with this?" I asked.

"You lay it down in the middle. Make sure its head is sticking out of the coil, though," she instructed. "You have to be the one to lay the snake down, since you're the one making the contract."

"Got it," I said, doing exactly as asked.

"Okay, before you start the chant, I need to let you know," she said, "you can't back out of this once the ritual is complete. They'll kill you if you try."

"I'm not planning on backing out," I said, focused on the satanic image in front of me.

"Okay, repeat after me, then. Say this six times, and then you wait."

She announced a quick chant, closing her eyes in the process. It sickened me that she knew this, but I had to kill Mark. If she didn't know about the Hellstitchers, Mark would have to go to prison, but knowing him, he'd try and wiggle his way out somehow. If he managed to succeed, my life would be over.

I repeated the chant Cherry gave me. I spoke it six times, all with my eyes closed. I felt my skin grow cold, and I heard a demonic laughter in the distance. My heartbeat sped up. I opened my eyes to see the pentagram was glowing a bright red. Wind started picking up in the middle of the room.

"It's working," Cherry said, her long blond hair flying in the breeze. "Just one more thing. You're the only one who can communicate with them. I can't see them or hear them."

I nodded to her, waiting for the Hellstitcher to appear. My heart was beating even faster now, just urging to jump out of my chest. Sweat dripped down the side of my bruised face, and silence filled the air in a matter of seconds. I then heard Cherry's grandfather clock ticking away in the other room. It was so loud. *Tick-tick-tick-tick-tick.* That's all I could hear. Cherry said something to me, but it was drowned out by the sound of the clock. *Tick-tick-tick-tick-tick.* My heart was racing at the speed of sound. *Tick-tick-tick-tick-tick.* A drop of sweat landed on my leg. *Tick-tick-tick-tick-tick.* My mouth grew dry. I was waiting a lifetime for the Hellstitcher. *Tick-tick-tick-tick-tick.*

The pentagram's light faded.

"He's here," Cherry whispered.

A swirl of blood erupted from the pentagram. From it, one large gray hand came out and propped itself to the floor. It was followed by another hand, then the two lifted the enormous body of an ashy demon out of the portal. He was huge, and he was frightening. He had piercing white eyes that seemed to stare into my very soul. I breathed heavily in his presence. I could not control my nervousness.

"Good evening, Monica," he said with the deepest voice unknown to man.

"H-hi," I said, putting a hand up. "Um, a-are you here to kill someone...for me?"

"Yes, I am. And you are willing to give up your soul for this dirty deed?"

"Yes," I said, straightening myself out. "But before I do that, can I ask you some questions? I'm really quite fascinated by your kind."

Cherry looked at me with a confused face. Her expressions were being ignored.

"Eh, sure," he answered. "Always a pleasure to speak with fans of our work."

"G-great," I said. I started asking simple questions first before moving on in detail. I had to remember all of this and write it down as soon as he left. With all the information he's giving me, I'd bet I could write an entire book with it. He sure enjoyed talking.

After a good twenty minutes of questions, he finally stopped me.

"Listen, lady, I've got a job to do," he said. "As much as I'd like to sit here and talk about my home, I don't want to keep this contract waiting."

"I understand," I replied, sadly lowering my head.

"Now, who's going to die tonight?" he asked eagerly.

"My husband," I said loudly. "The man is horrid, and you have to do this quickly. My parents' lives are at stake."

Cherry looked at me again with shock this time. She mouthed words to me, but I couldn't grasp what she was trying to say.

"If you want it done quickly, you can tell me what sort of items he loves," he said with crossed arms.

"Right, your killing methods are very strange, aren't they?" I said nervously. "Once you find him, he's always wearing our wedding ring. There's not a moment he's not wearing it. I think he's always loved it more than he has me. It has a big, raw, uncut diamond in it. That'll work."

"And a name?"

"Mark. Mark A—"

Chapter Fourteen

DEVIOUS

"So that's what started this all?" I asked. "You were raped by your abusive husband, and you took it upon yourself to have him dead?"

"That's what I said," Monica replied depressingly. "The cops showed up to my door later that night and told me he got T-boned. I felt like I never even sold my soul to begin with. The joy that came out of me was frightening to the police officer."

I was unfamiliar with the emotion I was feeling; I felt a little sorry for the old lady. Although she was enduring an eternity in Hell, I would have to guess she preferred it over being stuck with her husband. Regardless of how I was starting to feel, I needed to finish my job on the doctor. He still wanted me dead.

"Your story made me realize how much this really meant to you," I said firmly. "The extinction of the Hellstitchers is all you want, as some sort of redemption for selling your soul."

"I didn't have a choice, Hellstitcher," she said, tears falling. "He was an evil man. God knows what would've gone down if I hadn't killed him. Our kids—"

She stopped mid-sentence and began to cry again. I couldn't know what she felt, but at the same time, it was as if all her pain was leaching onto me. I need to get out of here, but I had one more question for her.

"Monica. Your son tells me only another demonic weapon can kill a Hellstitcher," I said softly. "Is this true?"

"My boy..." She whimpered. "Of course. I'm so happy he figured it out. In all of my years of research, I couldn't find the answer to that. But my son... He's done it. It's so simple."

"Wonderful."

"I'll bet that's the only way to kill your boss, too," she continued on. "Of course it's only theory, but with enough power, I'm sure it could rupture his organs and kill him all the same."

"We're done here."

I got up and began walking away. I wanted to leave Monica out of the river for now, just to spare her a few more minutes of suffering, but I knew I couldn't keep her out. If Satan happened to come by, he could interrogate her just as I did. I couldn't let him know there's a secret way to kill a Hellstitcher or even himself. If Monica's theory worked, I just may be able to walk out of this situation victorious.

I trotted back to Monica, sighing on the way. With one swift push, I tossed her back into the Sanguine River, ignoring the screams spewing out from her soul. My secret was safe from the Devil's grasp.

I made my way out of the library before realizing I had forgotten something. The Librarian kept records of everyone who'd been fished out. If Satan came looking, he'd find exactly what he's looking for.

Knowing it was the last time I could spend a

minute in Hell without being attacked, I pulled the doctor's gun out from my satchel. I stood in the doorway to the library, facing only the Silent Librarian. She was focusing on her meal.

In a matter of exactly six seconds, a beam of white light shot out from my weapon, and the Librarian fell from her perch, cracking the stone floor as it made contact. Smoke bogged out of the gaping hole I formed in her torso. It was a shame to see her go, especially after knowing her for hundreds of years. I looked down at her corpse in disappointment, knowing full well what was to come.

Making my way to the books, I snatched every single one of them and piled them up in the middle of the clean, stone-cut floor. A single shot of lava from my hand covered the pile, instantly causing them to combust. The records were all gone. The Library of the Damned was dead.

I exited the burning library, still feeling sour about losing it. I had to go to the throne before anything else. I could mess with Satan one last time... If I pretended to be hiding something, he'd freak out and search the library himself. He'd be searching for nothing. Besides, even if I told him the truth, he didn't trust me enough to take my word for it. He'd search the library anyway. I may as well make him look like a fool while he's at it.

I started sprinting up the cobblestone path, up to the bridge leading to the throne. It only took a matter of seconds, thanks to my incredible athletic body. Finding the Devil talking with the other three Hellstitchers, I immediately interrupted their conversation.

"My lord! I have bad news!" I yelled out, pushing my brothers out of my way.

"Be patient, Decipere!" Satan yelled in an annoyed tone of voice. "I am discussing something important with the other Hellstitchers."

"I can see that, but I felt you wanted to hear this, as it is rather urgent," I argued back.

"Out with it, then!" he spat. "What is *so* important that you had to push your brethren out of the way?"

"The man's mother had nothing new to tell me," I began. "Except for the fact she wants you dead, too."

"Right..." he said, yawning. "How is this important?"

"What do you mean?" I asked, kneeling down. "If she wants you dead, too, there could be a way her son can achieve that. Why kill only the Hellstitchers when you can strive to kill their creator, too?"

"What are you talking about, Decipere?" I heard Atrocify say. "Who in their right minds would even think about attacking us?"

"It's my contract, Atrocify. They set me up to die."

"That's impossible!" he said in disbelief. "Humans haven't been able to kill us within the last hundreds of years. How can they suddenly kill us now?"

"It's just one man, but he is determined. He claims to be making a special weapon, and I don't want to find out if it really works or not."

"Wait..." Immolatus hesitated. "If that's what's going on, what happen—"

"Immolatus!" I blurted out, knowing exactly

what he was about to say. "I have no more time to discuss this issue! It was a mistake even wasting time searching for a dead end."

Lucifer only squinted at me in a suspicious stare. He was silent for a few moments before finally sending me on my way.

"Very well, then," he said. "I suppose you want to go and finish your contract?"

"That is correct," I said, bringing myself to my feet once again.

"Go, then."

I quickly strode to my bloodportal. I was sure this caught his suspicions enough. And if he really did check the library, this bloodportal wouldn't be safe for me to travel through anymore. I knew he thought he's too smart for me, but when I came back to kill him, I'd be as safe as I could get.

The old man would have to comply to make me my final weapon. I would have it done within a day, or this would all be for nothing. I stepped into the bloodportal for the final time and disappeared.

Chapter Fifteen

I watched in disgust as Decipere left through his portal. The lazy fool was hiding something, and I planned to wash it out. The rest of the Hellstitchers resumed their discussion, but Tenebris was still nowhere to be found. I could only suspect something sinister happened to him.

As the ruler of Hell for the entirety of my existence as a fallen angel, it was my job to protect my most valuable agents, so long as they were obedient to me. Decipere was my Monger, yet he was the most disobedient of them all. He'd let his power go to his head a long time ago, and he believed he could take over my job as the dictator of Hell. I knew better.

If he's hiding something from me, it'd be found in the library. It could be his secret method of bringing me to my knees, but what could that even be? If he was telling the truth, he'd be quite lucky to be alive. I'd even consider helping him complete his contract, just to remind him he wasn't as powerful as he thought.

"Hellstitchers," I announced. "Do you put your trust in Decipere?"

"He is our brother," Atrocify replied. "He's never gone out of his way to harm us, unless it's to make a fool out of Tenebris. I don't exactly trust him, but I wouldn't expect him to turn on us."

"I believe he would," Immolatus butted in. "Maybe just to, yet again, prove to everyone how 'worthy' he is."

"You make sense. But would he really kill us? Would he not simply try and make us submit to him?"

"That still qualifies as turning on us," Immolatus argued, crossing his arms. "And if we resisted, he'd kill us for sure."

"Decipere not crazy!" Gomorrah yelled. "He is leader! He knows best!"

"He's not the best leader, Gomorrah," Atrocify said. "He doesn't seem to care about anyone but himself. Like I said, he doesn't go out of his way to harm us, but I don't trust him to help us if we need it. If it was Tenebris, he'd make an effort to make matters worse for him."

"We don't even *know* where Tenebris is," I said, rubbing my temples. "For all we know, Decipere could've tied him to some wall and left him there."

"Sire, that's what I tried to discuss when Decipere *showed* up," Immolatus said, worried. "Atrocify doesn't remember seeing Tenebris within the last day, but Gomorrah and I do."

"Go on."

"We were in the coliseum, having a practice battle for an upcoming tournament we were planning. Gomorrah got hurt and left, but I stayed in the arena. It was only a minute later where Decipere took Tenebris out of the arena and ordered an entire fifty demons to join in and occupy me. I assumed Decipere was only making fun of me at first, but when Tenebris' name popped up, I realized I hadn't seen him since."

"What?!" I yelled, eyes widening. My flowing rivers of lava picked up speed as my anger level started to rise. "So he pitted fifty demons against you just so he could keep you busy?"

"Decipere killed him, my lord!" he exclaimed. "I didn't think anything of it, but if Decipere is talking about some human who could kill Hellstitchers, we have to assume Tenebris is dead!"

"Decipere is dead, too!" I roared, getting up from my throne. "We're going to the library! If he found a way to kill me, we will find it, too!"

"Sire, what's our plan to stop Decipere from killing the rest of us or you?" Atrocify asked, speeding up along with me.

"My legion will deal with him!" I replied with rage.

We made our way to the Library of the Damned in a hasty fashion, quickly noticing smoke billowing out from it. Decipere had betrayed me.

I burst open the door with a foul kick. Inside, a flaming pile of books covered in lava took the spotlight in the middle of the floor. Millions of emotions filled my head as I resisted destroying the whole cave in sheer anger.

"Lucifer, the Librarian is dead!" Atrocify pointed out. "She has a strange marking surrounding her wound."

I circled the book pile to find the Librarian collapsed. She had white veins growing around the crisp hole in her stomach. My precious daughter was dead. Killed by my Monger. My highest-ranking official was Hell's own snake, and he shall die for his sins.

"Our leader..." Immolatus muttered. "Our

brother, he killed one of our own and slaughtered the Librarian...just to make sure there weren't any loose ends?"

"Yes, brother," Atrocify groaned back. "As a demon, it seems wrong to feel such betrayal. But I can't help feeling so empty."

"I thought he'd grow out of his ego," he said back. "It may have taken another thousand years, but it'd be worth it to have a leader that cared."

"Sad," Gomorrah joined in. "Angry and sad. I want punishment."

Immolatus gave a long sigh. He continued staring at the burning pile of records, knowing the library's time was over. His vivid white eyes seemed to shift into an iridescent gray, clouding what joy he had left.

"Atrocify," I spoke, fingers twitching.

"Yes, sire?" he said, kneeling down.

"Rally up the legion. Order them to meet their malevolent ruler at his throne."

"I understand."

Atrocify darted out of the library, leaving only Gomorrah and Immolatus with me. Gomorrah was weeping at the pile of destroyed records, while Immolatus attempted to find records left untouched.

"Gomorrah! Immolatus!" I called. The two found their way to me immediately, Gomorrah still groaning. "You're coming to the throne with me. When Atrocify gets there, tell him you all will encircle Decipere's bloodportal and strike him the moment he walks through."

"My lord, Decipere may expect us to wait there. He could be ready."

"You will be backed up by the legion. He cannot fight all of you at once; he's not as strong as he makes himself believe."

We burst out of the library with a loud bang. I was furious at my fallen soldier, and he was going to face the wrath of his maker!

I ordered the other two Hellstitchers to my side and started up the path back to my throne. Every step we took shook the entire cave; stalactites crumbled at the pressure of my monstrous stomps.

At a snail's pace, we began to see demons emerge from their own personal caves. They knew what was to come. Shrieks and cries echoed throughout Hell as more and more demons charged up to the throne. By the time I arrived, I had my army waiting for their orders.

"Legion of Hell!" I announced, raising my hands up. "Today you face a new enemy, one that you have never dreamed of fighting before."

The ocean of demons before me was enormous. Their cheering and screeching was all that could be heard. Demons were flying, standing, and crawling up the walls of Hell, all surrounding my throne. I needed all the protection I could get; Decipere would have a weapon capable of killing me. My first line of defense was the remaining three Hellstitchers, surrounding the bloodportal that brought Decipere in. My second line of defense was the legion, with its waves upon waves of warriors ready to strike down any being unfortunate enough to cross them. I was the last line of defense. If Decipere managed to get through everything else, I'd blow him away with the unholiest of fires imaginable. I would utterly decimate him.

"My most trusted advisor, my Monger, has betrayed us!" I yelled to the crowd. "He will have a weapon capable of killing me, and he intends to use it as soon as he gets the chance! Decipere will have no chance at stopping us all! He will falter at our strength!"

The legion cheered on, eventually forming a chant.

"Her-e-tic! Her-e-tic! Her-e-tic!"

"No, he is no heretic!" I yelled again. "He is but a traitor to me, to you, to all of us! He believes he is the true leader of Hell, and he will bend you all to his own will if he gets his way! But we are nigh invincible together, and that shall not happen!"

I swung a fist to the sky with a mighty roar. The crowd followed my movements; they were ready. Decipere hadn't the slightest of chances. Soon he would be dead, and Atrocify would be my new Monger. I would make two new Hellstitchers to replace him and Tenebris, and they would bend to my very will. I would have complete domination.

"He will show up any minute!" I said, settling down the audience. "Be on your guard, and don't let him get past my Hellstitchers."

I walked over my crazed army, carefully making sure I didn't squash any demon ignorant enough to lie under my foot. Soon enough, I got to my throne and sat down in a kingly position. The clock was ticking, and I was ready.

***

Hours went by waiting for Decipere to return from his bloodportal. The more we waited, the more agitated I got. Smoke was streaming from my nose, and my lava currents were flowing faster and faster. I could rip a skyscraper in half with just a fraction of my rage.

"My lord," Atrocify spoke. "Is there a chance he comes in through the main gate to Hell? This could be a trap. He wouldn't have set the library on fire if it wasn't."

"Decipere tried to lie, thinking I would believe him," I replied, ignoring him. "He's only playing mind games. Unfortunately for him, he will lose."

"Okay, and what is your plan if he *does* come through the main entrance?"

"Hmm..." I thought. "Given the circumstances, it's highly unlikely he'd do such a thing. It's a long way to the throne from there, and he'd have to get past Cerberus before even stepping foot into Hell."

"This is Decipere we're dealing with. He's the Monger for a reason. He could even take a bloodportal to the very entrance of Hell and not have to fight Cerberus."

"Okay, Atrocify," I said, fed up. "I have already sealed Hell of future bloodportal openings from the outside. This one by the throne is the only one he can use. If he manages to come through the main entrance, I have a plan."

"That's very good. What is it?"

As if on cue, I glanced toward the entrance of my realm and noticed the giant gate had been opened. I stood up and spotted Decipere trudging along the rocks, making his way to my location. The bastard tricked me. He made me his fool.

I growled in an unholy amount of steam and roared to the winds.

"Kill him!" I spat, shooting my gigantic finger up.

One by one, demon after demon, my army rose to the sky and rocketed toward the Monger. The other three Hellstitchers picked their weapons up and went to follow behind them, but I stopped them in their tracks.

"You three!" I growled. "You're staying up here in case he tries pulling a portal trick out of his ass."

"Why not send just me?" Atrocify asked with a bow. "Immolatus and Gomorrah are suitable for defending you if he attempts such a move."

"You're all staying up here," I backfired. "Once he's been tired out by the legion, you will all have your full strength to do battle with him. I need that of you."

"Understood!" he replied with haste. "You ordered the legion to kill him, but do you really believe they'll be able to?"

"Oh yes, my demons are well-fit to kill, even if it is my own Monger. He's already been weakened by our guardian, Cerberus. He won't be able to fight much longer."

"And if they fail?"

I gave Atrocify a wretched disapproving look.

"If they fail, I will have you three take him out!" I bellowed.

"He has a weapon that can annihilate both you and us," Immolatus blurted out. "I suggest we interrogate Decipere about the ins and outs of it and see if we can destroy it without accidentally killing ourselves. It'll be worth it to know what kind of power he has."

"I like your idea," I said in a calm manner. "Fine!

You three will bring him to me alive. Do whatever is necessary to get him here. Cut his limbs off, knock him out, tie him up, it doesn't matter. Do you understand?"

"Yes, my lord!" Immolatus and Atrocify said in unison.

Gomorrah stood watching the battle, seemingly not paying attention to a single word we had just discussed. I bent over and gave him a quick shove to see if he actually knew what was going on or not.

"Yes, lord, I understand," he said at last. "I will ensnare him in my sulfur trap."

"Good," I said, resting my arms down. "Now we wait."

Chapter Sixteen

DESPERATE

I landed back at my target's lawn. The air was still and dry, and the only audible sounds were those of the crickets. The scent of wood and cut grass piled together into my nostrils, and the dirt below my feet was rigid and stiff. This was it. I had used my throne-bloodportal for the last time, and I had to close it off.

With closed eyes, I grasped the rim of my portal and forced it closed. It made a squelching sound as it disappeared from the air, followed by a splash of blood onto the grass below it.

I had one shot at making this work. Once I'd forced the doctor to make me a new weapon, I'd have to kill him before my time was up. Facing the reality of the situation, I doubted there was enough time to make it happen. If the doctor died without giving me a means to kill the Devil, I'd have to stay on Earth for the rest of my existence, just to keep myself alive.

I had a plan, however, and it relied on the time of day. I opened my satchel up to check my Rolex, seeing that it was 5:46. Excellent. I had a few moments to gather my thoughts before I executed the plan. Once I got into the house, I'd have to follow through.

I sat silently in the grass, watching the trees

around the house sway in the slow wind. Every couple of minutes, I checked back on my golden Rolex, waiting for it to hit the right time. Intensively staring at it, I reminisced on the moment I claimed it. The boy I stole it from deserved his fate. I never felt happier demolishing a human life, but now that I had this watch in my hands, I realized there was a more efficient way to shut him up. Perhaps I wouldn't have had to go on a car chase if I only knew self-control.

Snapping me back to reality, the Rolex hit 5:50. It was time. I got up from the ground, wiping the dirt from my legs. Step by step, I approached the doctor's humble abode. Standing on the porch, I gave a chuckle at the door opposing me. With a giant kick, I flung the door straight off the hinges and made my way inside. The doctor came running out from behind a corner, seeing that I was back for more.

"You! Get out of my house!" he yelled, pointing a finger at me. "Haven't you taken enough from me?"

"I haven't taken nearly enough from you!" I fired back. "Once I take your life, I will be all but satisfied."

"You can't kill me even if you tried," he said, breathing heavily. "There's nothing you can do."

"We're going to get to that in a moment, old man," I said, leaning on the wall. "Right now, I need you to make me a weapon that can kill my overlord."

"What? Why would I make that for you, after what you did?"

"Because if you don't, I will destroy your life, ruining everything and everyone around you until you submit. You will have no choice!"

"As if I'm supposed to believe that," he said, turning away. "You have less than a day to kill me before you shrink into a pathetic waste of a demon. Besides, I have no idea how to kill your boss."

"Your mother tells me he can be killed the same way a Hellstitcher can, if it had enough power applied. And yes, you *will* make me this weapon in that time frame."

"My mother?!" he yelled, completely ignoring my demand. "You talked to my mother?"

"Yes, she was in our library," I bragged. "She's living a very heinous life in eternity."

"You—" the doctor started before stopping himself. "That's absurdly uncalled for."

"How so? It was quite lovely to meet her."

"It was manipulative! It was controlling!" he exclaimed. "You had no right going to her!"

"I had all the right I wanted, Baldy!" I replied, smirking. "Not only that, but I learned why your mother summoned a Hellstitcher in the first place."

"I'm sure it was just to get rid of you abominations."

"No, no, no..." I began. "She never even *knew* the Hellstitchers existed until she had to call one."

This struck his curiosity. He was latched on, determined to find the answer. His bright blue eyes shined bright as he peered into mine. The most important piece of history from his mother that he didn't know already was like a treasure; he simply had to know.

"Tell me," he said in a tame voice.

"Oh, I don't think I can," I said in a sarcastic tone. "Maybe I'll let you in on a few tidbits, but ultimately, you're only going to know the whole story if you make me this new weapon."

"You can forget it, then."

"I won't, and you won't forget it, either," I said luringly. "This is what started your little quest in the first place. If you don't know why exactly you're working on it, why *are* you working on it?"

"I'm fulfilling my mother's wishes because I agree with her," he began. "She believes the Hellstitchers are beings of pure evil that need to be destroyed at all cost. They're workers of Satan, and that is unforgivable."

"We exist out of Satan's wishes. That is fact, and we have no control over it. We are who we were made to be. I was made to be the best out of all of us! Your mother had much more to the story than just believing we were bad. She had no choice but to call upon us, unless she wanted to risk the safety of *all* of her loved ones."

"I don't believe you, Decipere," he said with a sigh. "You're a liar and a deceiver. How can I trust anything you say? You lied to me about the Monger, you got your own family member killed, and you stole my gold coin!"

"You gave that worthless coin to me!" I yelled. "And you *have* to believe me! There's not another single being on the planet, nor in Hell, that can recover your mother's story."

"If you're the only option, I don't want it," he argued back. "No matter how curious I am, I won't let you fool me again. It's not happening."

"Huh," I grunted. "So you wouldn't believe me if I told you your mother was beaten and raped? By her own husband, at that?"

"I-I..." he stuttered. "I wouldn't believe you, no."

"How unfortunate. That's exactly what happened, and it was ongoing for four months. She got pregnant with you during that time."

"How unbelievable you are, Decipere. It's amazing."

"It's all true, old coot!" I said in frustration. "You've got no one better to believe!"

"If that's the case, it's not worth even hearing," the doctor said. "It's inappropriate that you were even able to talk to her in the first place."

"I don't care if it was the worst act in history. It's already done. Now, I have your weapon in my satchel right now, and you will upgrade it to kill the Devil!"

"I don't need to upgrade jack!" he asserted.

"You will! Or there will be consequences!"

"If what my mother says is true, you already have a way to make that weapon kill him!"

"What?" I paused, confused. What could he possibly mean by this? "What are you talking about?"

"Oh, I'm so sorry. Should I be more specific? Is that what you want?"

"Yes, it is!" I growled, punching a hole in his wall. "Tell me this instant!"

"Make me, Hellstitcher," he said in a dominant tone. "With the last bit of time you have, make me."

I yelled out in anger, ripping up the carpeted floor beneath me. Within seconds, I tore the entire carpet off of the base and burned it to a crisp. No ashy cloud shot out of its cinders, much to my dismay.

"Forget it. I'll figure it out myself!" I yelled, suddenly throwing furniture over in a berserk fit.

"You need to leave now, Decipere! Leave me and my daughter alone! There's nothing else you can gain from me."

"I know damn well you want to make another weapon, Doc!" I shouted. "I am not letting you win! I will find whatever means necessary to end your miserable life!"

"You can't do that, Decipere!" he cried out with a smirk. "I've already told you, there's nothing you can do to kill me!"

"Just watch me!" I called, razing everything in sight. I swiftly went around the room, incinerating everything I made contact with. The decorations, the furniture, the tools, all of it was being destroyed. All the while I still tried to comprehend what the doctor meant. Despite the amount I was burning, I still failed to hear any screech rise out of the ashes, along with a darkened black cloud. This doctor meant exactly what he said.

After completely emptying three rooms of the house, I ran back to the doctor and knocked him to the floor. I pulled the Rolex out of my satchel to see it was 5:59. It was time for my last resort.

"I...will *end* you!" I said, breathing heavily.

"You've lost, Decipere." The doctor laughed. "You have nothing to kill me with, and you will fail at the job you were best at!"

"You are gravely mistaken, old man," I said, getting a puzzled look from him. "I have but one thing that can kill you."

"Try me, asshole."

I laughed at his remark. He would soon pay for his foolishness in the most appropriate of manners. All he must do was come to the final conclusion of my plan. I laughed and laughed and laughed before forcing myself to simmer down.

"Look at the time," I said excitedly.

He continued to stare at me, perplexed by my answer. Only a moment later, he realized what I had been preparing the entire time. In less than a second, he got to his feet.

"Lila! Lila!" he called, running out of the room.

"Go ahead! I'll give you a head start!" I yelled, laughing all the while.

I turned around and ran out of the house to see the doctor had caught up with his daughter, just now getting home. He was speaking to his daughter very quickly, Lila looking just as puzzled as the doctor was just a minute before. The doctor gave a rapid glance to me, speeding up his talk.

I gave a mighty roar and charged at him and his daughter, snatching her up into my giant yellow hands. Lila screamed for her father at the top of her lungs. I ran to the porch and stood at the top of the stairs, holding her up to the sky. Lila struggled in my hands, trying desperately to break free.

"Daddy! Help! What's happening?" she cried out.

"Let her go, Decipere!" he yelled, face turning a deep red. "Let go of my daughter! It's going to be okay, Munchkin!"

"Your daughter is now your motivation!" I shouted with a smile. "If you won't tell me how to kill you properly, just conside—"

I froze, letting out a deep gasp. The doctor held the weapon up in both hands, starting the charge up to the blast. In my utter shock, I completely let go of the fact I was holding his daughter. I dropped her from my hands, beginning a countdown in my head. It felt like slow motion as I counted the seconds down.

Six. Lila hit the wooden floor, climbing to her feet at an instant. Five. She took off running, arms out for her father. Four. I realized what had happened and quickly looked around me. Three. I grabbed the two wooden pillars at my sides, tearing them each off of the porch. Two. I leaped to the Earth, running for my target. One. My two beams of wood made their way into the flesh, instantly impaling the poor soul in front of me. It was Lila.

Chapter Seventeen

REGRET

Silence had befallen the three of us. I was rising the two stakes into the sky, both beholding the child of my enemy. The sun was especially bright today, its rays shining down at the perfect point to give me a silhouette of my victim. I couldn't keep my eyes off it.

Blood slowly ran down the stakes and onto my hands. They were both stuck inside the girl's stomach, one directly in the middle and one right next to it but slightly elevated. I finally gained control of my breath and turned my gaze to the doctor. He was mortified.

The gun was tilted in his hands, now shaking from the horrific sight that beheld him. His mouth was slightly dropped open in disbelief, but nothing came out of it. Sweat dripped down the sides of his cheeks before his eyes started watering. His skin turned pale as a ghost.

Suddenly, the gun dropped from his hands onto his freshly mowed lawn. With it, his violently shaking hands also slowly fell to his sides. His jaw began shaking, as if he were trying to say something.

Weak sounds of pain uttered from above. The little girl was groaning out for her father. Blood dripped down from her mouth, finding its place on my chest.

I bent down and forced one stake into the

ground, forcing more painful moans from Lila. I forced the other one into the earth below, giving it a stable ground to stand on. Lila choked and coughed up a river of blood, still muttering for her father.

"Da..." she groaned. Her legs lay down still, but her fingers were twitching in a peculiar movement, as if they were trying to grab something.

"Da..." she said again. Her father only stood a few yards away, still staring at his dying daughter. Rivers and rivers of tears were falling from his bloodshot eyes.

With my heart beating a hundred miles a minute, I slowly walked to him. I stood at his side, but he refused to look away from his daughter. I could hear his erratic breathing; it was as if he was using all his energy to keep himself from crying out on the spot.

I looked back at Lila. She was still groaning in intervals. Her body hung from the wooden stakes in the coldest way imaginable. Her hand was finally making full movements, still struggling to grasp thin air.

"Dadth..." she uttered before coughing up more blood. Tears were mixing with the copious amount of blood leaving her mouth. Her eyes were fixed on me, but I knew she couldn't see me. Still, it felt as if she knew I was staring back. Her silent eyes spoke a thousand words, yet nothing could be understood. The longer she peered into me, the more regret I felt. It was unspeakable.

I turned my head to the weapon the doctor dropped, trying to get the thought of her staring at me out of my head. I quickly picked it up and took a few steps away. My body was turned to the woods, but I only saw Lila's face. I held the gun in my hands with only the thought of her in my mind. One look at my gun told me just how despicable I was. I could see my own reflection in its glossy white coat. All I could see, then, was a horrific beast.

I let the weapon drop to the ground a second time before turning back to the bloody scene. The doctor was still staring in shock, and Lila was still groaning and grasping for nothing.

Moments later, the doctor dropped to his knees and clenched his teeth. He made audible grunts, trying his hardest not to burst out in cries of sorrow. He slowly dragged his knees across the yard, making his way to his daughter. When he finally reached her, he held her hand, stopping it from continuing to grab nothing.

"Dad..." she cried, face turning red. Her expressions were nothing short of tragic.

"H-hi...Munchkin..." he stuttered out. Nothing could ever hide the tears that fell from his eyes.

"Dadthy..." she groaned again.

"I-I-I'm here, L-Lila," he said. "I'm here."

"Dadth...hurts..." She whimpered. "Hurts... Hurts... Hurts... Hurts..."

"I know i-it-it hurts, Lila—"

He was suddenly cut off by the coughing up of more blood, making it drip all over his lab coat. He did not care. I could only feel more guilty by the second.

"I-I love you, M-Munchkin," he whispered.

"Dadthy..." she cried. "Lo-o-ove..."

"I'm sorry, Lila... I'm so sorry. I'm so sorry."

"Uhh..." she said, tears stopping their flow.

"Lila!" her father cried, trying to force a smile. "H-hey. Hold on to...my heart, Lila. O-Okay?"

He placed his daughter's hand over his chest, singing to her.

"If you put your hand on me, I'll hold on to you.

If you hold on to my heart, I'll hold on to you.

If you leave me for a day or two, I'll hold on to you.

If I leave you for a day or two, I'll return to you.

Nothing ever changes, I'll keep you in my hand.

I'll hold on to y—"

He stopped himself as he started crying too hard. The two only cried with each other, until Lila finally spoke back.

"I'm," she uttered. "Hol-ding. O-o-o-o-n."

The doctor suddenly burst out loud, crying in his daughter's hand. He held her close as she continued groaning and coughing. Eventually, she stopped coughing and started taking deep breaths. One last shudder came from her lips as her entire body went completely limp. A black, ashy cloud exited her mouth, followed by the cry of a child. Moments later, the doctor looked to the sky with a final tear and slumped over. His hand was still wrapped around Lila's. Smoke leaked out of his nose and mouth. My contract...was over.

I was full of immense, foreign emotions. I only stood watching the two bodies as thoughts raced through my own mind. Guilt, anger, regret, self-hatred, and sadness. That was all going on. I couldn't help but feel *this*, and nothing else. I realized now how much of a monster I was. I was a villain, and I was always the villain. Both villain and monster, that's who

I was. And I couldn't be more disappointed.

***

All night I waited there, just watching the two bodies lie in ruin. I could only think of what I'd done to get here and what I could've done to avoid this. Thinking about this would never bring them back to life, but it's all I *could* think of.

The doctor was trying to kill me; I had to act quickly! What else could I have done? How could I have known he snatched the weapon from my satchel when I wasn't looking? I had no alternatives. I either killed them or died! I had to do it. I had to!

What if I didn't have to? What if I just left Lila out of it? What if I searched the whole planet for something to kill the doctor with? What if I just accepted my fate and let the doctor kill me? He would have killed us all. That's what he felt was right. The world was corrupted with sin, and the Hellstitchers made it worse.

It didn't matter. None of it mattered anymore. The man was dead. His daughter was dead. I was at fault for both of them. As the offender, I deserved a punishment. I could not allow an evil such as myself to roam around on his own free will. He did not deserve that. *I* did not deserve that.

After slumping my head all night, I finally lifted it back up, realizing what I had to do. The doctor's mission was to finish off the Hellstitchers; therefore I was now in charge of his quest. I was the one who had to do it. There was no one else strong enough or fast enough to do what must be done.

I stood up, still looking at the horrendous mess in front of me. Over the night, I continued to wonder what the doctor meant when he told me I already had the means to kill Satan, but looking back over my options, I realized just what he was saying. The weapon alone wasn't powerful enough to kill Satan, of course. It would be saved, however, until I met him.

I hesitated walking away, still looking back at the two. My disgusting deed would be forever trapped within my mind. I would not go a day without thinking about it. Nevertheless, I had to go and finish what the doctor started all those years ago. I had to fulfill his and his mother's work. My destination was Hell, but I needed to fight its guardian before I could get back in.

Chapter Eighteen

VICIOUS

The bloodportal opened in front of me. It would not take me to Hell, but it'd take me close. I stared into the bloody depths of my portal for a millennium. It could be the last time I used one. Its swirling crimson mist soothed my nostrils, and its sight was truly captivating. All night I could stay here, only watching the portal.

I had gotten everything I needed. And now, I would accomplish what I longed to do at the very beginning. After everything that'd happened, I felt the reasoning was entirely different this time.

I broke focus and looked down, searching for the doctor's weapon. There it was, only a few feet away from me. After claiming it once again, I put it in my satchel and took a step in my bloodportal. Its watery texture melted my skin with pleasure. Knowing it could be the last I felt of it, I knew I had to savor every moment.

***

I wound up in an unfamiliar land. Steam rose from cracks within the red, stony ground. Stalactites littered the ceiling above me, and ashy geysers covered much of the land around. This was near the entrance to Hell, near Cerberus.

I wandered around the foreign land, observing various debris floating in the air. Strange creatures were occasionally spotted trotting along another path. I never saw these creatures on Earth, but I felt the need to approach one. I wanted to *touch* one.

The more I wandered, the more I doubted myself. I'd been wandering for perhaps twenty minutes, but I hadn't seen any such sign of Hell nearby. The path I was on was the correct one; I was positive of it.

While on my journey, the events leading up to this moment passed through my memories, again and again. I'd killed too many people, and I'd destroyed so many lives, just out of sheer boredom. Many of them weren't even contracts; I simply ruined the lives of innocents because I wanted to. Words could not describe how much I regretted it. Forgiveness was not an option for me, and no matter how many people I helped, forgiveness would never *be* an option. I didn't deserve it. I could not atone for my crimes, and for that, I must pay somehow.

One thing I could do, however, was fulfill the doctor's mission. Completing his goal would be the only way I could make up for a small section of my actions. The other Hellstitchers would die, the entire legion of demons would die, Satan would die, and Cerberus would die. That left no sort of demonic entities alive, save for myself. Knowing I went beyond the doctor's goals would make him proud, if he and his daughter were still alive...

Those were just two of the people I'd destroyed. Not only them, but I murdered a stupid teenager, just because he disrespected me. I'd killed countless others and laughed in their faces when they died. I even tortured some of them, using a smoke bomb on them, just to get a little extra fun out of it. It was gut-wrenching.

I even killed one of my own. My brother, Tenebris...I could tell just how happy he was to work with me when I knew I was leading him to his death. He thought I finally saw worth in him, and he was so proud. It was the happiest I'd seen a demon be. I thought it to be revolting back then, but now that he's gone, I wished I could've saved him. All of the mistreating I'd done to him...all of the boasting, beating, yelling, and ignoring I'd done. Why did I like tormenting him, when all he wanted was my attention?

I continued trudging along the path, miserably thinking about the lives I'd screwed up. I soon saw a vermillion light coming from up ahead. Knowing those had to be the gates, I sped up my pace. The rocky ground soon turned to stone brick, smoothed out to ease the feet of travelers. As I got closer, a clear image finally formed. It was a skyscraper of a gate, carved into the cave wall. Torches of red lined the sides of the gates, as well as the cave walls around it. A big, hulking figure was standing directly in front of it, poised in a killer position. It was Cerberus.

The three-headed dog spotted me instantly, changing pose to face me instead. Cerberus was watching the gates twenty-four-seven. He never took a moment to rest, unless Satan called for it. For all of the years I'd been alive, he'd never had Cerberus paused from duty. The wretched dog had been guarding Hell for over a thousand years with no break whatsoever. I would end that.

Cerberus growled at me as I got closer. Soon I only came a hundred feet to him, and he looked agitated. Foam formed at his mouth, and all of his eyes were narrowed onto my person. His three heads were just as menacing as his fangs; a single bite could pierce my magma-like skin.

I put my hand to the hidden pocket on the back strap of my satchel. From there, I dragged my Jugulator out. Cerberus gave a smoky scoff, poising his body to strike once again. I pressed the switch on my morningstar, releasing the chain from the hilt. The spiky ball at the end fell to the ground, cracking the earth as it hit. Cerberus gave a warning bark before growling again. I chuckled and gripped my morningstar with all of my might.

Leaping toward the dog, I swung the morningstar to the left, barely scraping the dog's front paws. Cerberus had managed to dodge the attack and strike back with incredible force. He headbutted me to the sky and followed it up by jumping at my flying body. I swung my weapon to deflect his deadly bite.

I landed on my feet and rushed the dog again. I swung and swung with my morningstar, with Cerberus barely dodging every blow. He took a few strikes of his own, attempting bites at every side. My elbows quickly blocked his jaws between every swing of my weapon. I thought about pulling out the doctor's weapon, but I wasn't sure if it would have enough power if I used it too much. I had to save it for Satan.

Soon enough, I crushed one of Cerberus's front paws, and he jumped back in agony. He stopped and howled before leaping into battle again. Every blow drained my stamina even more; I could feel myself getting slower and slower every second. Cerberus dedicated his entire life to guarding Hell, but I would end it here, regardless of how weary I became.

Cerberus got ahold of my foot and swung me into a wall. My morningstar flew out of my hand thereafter. I was nearly defenseless, but I still had my fists and lava. I picked myself off the ground before realizing he was lunging toward me again. I managed to land a blow onto his middle head, but the left one grabbed me by the arm. I felt his teeth crunching down on my skin, but I stuck my giant hand into his nose and shot a burst of lava. Writhing in pain, he immediately dropped me to the ground and let another head have a go at me.

With a single stroke of skill, I jumped over the beast and yoinked it by the black hair of his head. Landing on its neck, I locked my arms and legs around his throat and squeezed to my fullest might. His other heads struggled to grab ahold of me as I slowly strangled the dog's right head. Within a few seconds, the head went limp, and blood poured out of his nose and leaked out of his eyes. One head down, two to go.

Cerberus finally got a grip and jumped on his back, knocking the wind out of me as he rolled my body off. The dog pouted for a moment, with the two of his remaining heads staring at the hanging one. Turning back to me, Cerberus bared his fangs and went for another round.

He took multiple shots at me, each being blocked by my arms. With the speed of his attacks, I still wasn't able to break free of his assault. He soon switched it up and caught me off guard, going for only a single leg of mine. He flung me to the ground before violently shaking me in the air, spinning my head around and around. He slammed me into the ground multiple times with each time bringing me to the sky to gain momentum. I was merely a ragdoll in his jaws. Gaining a new presence of mind, I grasped onto a rock as I hit the ground and held on as tight as possible. Cerberus yanked at my body, desperately trying to win the tug of war. He wouldn't let go of my leg and clenched his teeth even harder.

His teeth broke my skin. Fangs sunk into my flesh as he continued to pull me off of my rock. I yelped in pain as he only dug into more of my meat. My leg was bleeding furiously, but I couldn't help it. Thinking quickly, I launched myself off of the rock, throwing Cerberus back. My hands were able to hang onto his stubby snout, and I glared into his eyes with burning anger. Teeth clenched, I plunged both of my hands into his nostrils and shot gallons upon gallons of lava up his nose. I felt his grip on my leg loosen, and the dog finally let go. I fell to the ground a second later, lifting my head up to see Cerberus's left head was now completely dead. Smoke funneled out of every hole on his head, and lava oozed its way out of his nose and mouth. Just one to go.

The middle head went berserk, barking furiously and howling at his other head's loss. He rushed me, pinning me to the ground as he tried to fit me inside his entire mouth. I held the roof of his mouth with my hands as my one good leg held his jaw open. Knowing this was an opportunity, Cerberus shook his head in a violent manner, turning me dizzy once again. He paused for a moment before finally slamming me onto the top of a sharp rock.

My joints collapsed at my pain, and I fell into the mouth of Cerberus's final head. He attempted to chew me alive, but I held his teeth open as much as I could. This could not be how I went. Knowing exactly what to do, I doused even more lava out of my hands until Cerberus instantly spit me out of his mouth, along with the smoking-hot lava. He leaped at me again, but I was ready. With both fists, I stopped Cerberus dead in his tracks and punched his snout with maximum force. He barely flinched and lifted me onto his head. I tried a grab at his neck, but with the force of a thousand blows, he shot me up into the sky. I flew up until I hit the rocky ceiling above and hung onto a massive stalactite beside me. As I hung about two hundred feet above my enemy, an idea sparked in my head. Seeing another medium-sized stalactite just next to me, I snapped it off the stalk and let go of the bigger one. I was in a free fall.

Rapidly gaining speed, I closed in on the satanic dog below. He looked up at me in rage and leaped to catch me out of the sky. He failed.

With the timing just right, I swirled my body until I got a clear shot and sunk the broken stalactite into the dog's brain, killing it in an instant. I hit the floor with a loud thud but got to my feet at once. Cerberus let out one more whimper and collapsed. Drool flowed out of all of their mouths, creating a small puddle of disgusting spit. I said nothing and moved on.

Walking all over the land around, I searched for my morningstar. It's a shame it didn't help me against my fight against Cerberus, but I had a feeling it would be most optimal against what was to come. Finding it only after a minute of searching, I stood at the gates to Hell.

Before opening, I took another glance at Cerberus's corpse. I set down my Jugulator and strode back to it. I put my hand on the rough black fur covering the entirety of the body and started petting it.

"Good boy," I whispered. "You died doing your job. I am sorry it came to this."

After walking back to the gates, I broke it open with a monstrous kick and picked up my weapon. I was in.

Chapter Nineteen

PRIDE

I walked for several minutes. Step by step, my heart continued to beat faster. There was no going back from this. I walked with a hard limp, credit due to Cerberus. That damned dog may have sealed my fate against the rest of Satan's demons. The blazing heat of Hell frenzied my senses, and it surged the rush of blood flowing in my veins. Thoughts raced through my mind, and rage burned within my eyes. If I survived this, I would still be walking. Only then, it'd be toward nowhere.

A colossal "Kill him!" bellowed from the other end of Hell, letting me know Satan had spotted me. He wasn't planning on losing this fight at all. The entirety of Hell was at his side, and all I had were my wits and my morningstar. My beloved Jugulator was the one who'd been at my side since the very beginning. If there's any time at all it couldn't let me down, it's right now.

The demons rose to the sky, lances in hand. In unity, they grew into a wave of unstoppable force. The vast army of Hell, coming to slay the slayer. It's pathetic. A sea of red and black blotted out the path, but I kept walking. One more step, and then another. The screeches of the demonic creatures drew me in like a worm on a hook. I was taking that bait, but I was not going to be reeled in to my death.

A thought popped into my head, and I reached into my satchel. If every demon had left their post, perhaps I could take a bloodportal to the throne after all. I took my pair of binoculars and searched for Lucifer and his enormous chair. My portal was still being guarded, but by the other Hellstitchers. Their stakeout wasn't going anywhere, as long as there were still more soldiers to throw at me. Maybe if there were just a few demons guarding it, even ten, maybe I could bash my way through. Not with the Hellstitchers, though. Satan was making me put in all the work I could into getting what I need. Frustrated, I grunted and crushed the binoculars into the ground.

"Damn it!" I yelled. Growling, I began walking again.

More steps. More steps. Another few steps. The incomprehensible screams of the army were growing ever so close. They filled my ears and drowned my thoughts like a wave crashing into a ship. The ground below me felt of stone and dirt. Its rough texture comforted my bare feet. This ground would be my advantage, just as the air would be theirs. I clicked the button on my morningstar, letting the head break loose on its chain, and continued to drag it along the rocky terrain. I stared angrily at the demons while they closed in on my location, as the scrapes of the weapon I held sung a melody of destruction for whomever it made contact with.

I began to walk faster, and faster, and faster. My rage fueled the bigger steps I took toward the monstrous force of Hell. This desolate land would bring the culmination of their lives! They grew bigger, bigger, and bigger in my sights. And I grew yet into theirs. The palpable stench of burned blood already stained my nostrils, and my heart beat faster, and faster, and faster. Then, at the edge of the blade, I let out a crashing roar and threw myself into the depths of certain death!

My person was a storm, blowing away everything in its path! The demons didn't stand a chance against me. Blow by blow, my Jugulator crushed every red demonic limb and skull it touched. It was the instrument of my will, and my will was to *pulverize* anything in my path!

My body ebbed and flowed through the motions. The demons' blackened lances and tridents could not scrape me, but my malicious morningstar gave them a quick path to their demise. A flurry of deathly attacks came from my other hand, grabbing and horrifically crushing the torso of another soldier, then backhanding another's face, snapping their neck from the whiplash with a loud *CRUNCH.* I rolled and moved around as I needed, while most of the targets stayed in the air. I dodged their spear throws with ease and used their discarded weapons to my advantage, throwing them back toward the user or simply whacking the demons closer to me so that I could easily finish them off while they're stunned. If the crowd was having this much trouble even touching such a large target like me, how could they have any hope to slay the beast?

A lucky hit came from the prick next to me who I didn't see, getting a stab on my right hand. A jolt of panic struck me as the Jugulator dropped from my hand, but I immediately followed it up with grabbing the unfortunate abomination and began using him as my weapon instead. His body blunted against his cohorts, knocking them away or straight-up crushing them with the incalculable force I put into the blow. Bit by bit, his body fell apart the more I used it to kill the others. After only a few more seconds, all he became was a head with half of his torso. I tossed his disembodied corpse into the group, then lunged toward where he flew. The demons that it hit were on the ground, and I bashed their skulls into the rocks while they were still trying to react.

My weapon was gone and lost, and I had only my hands to deal the damage now. A demon leaped onto my back and attempted to stab his lance through my heart. I swiftly fell to the ground, crushing both him and his unworthy attempt. As I jumped back up, more demons charged into my face, my reflexes barely blowing them back. I continued to turn around and dodge attacks, weaving through the metal and blood. Fatigue was ready to grip me by the arm and pull me to the floor, but I wasn't giving in yet. I grabbed a group of three demons who were about to get the jump on me and blasted them away with the lava from my hands. I continued to use this burst of lava and melted the bodies of multiple enemies behind me. The lava flow suddenly ended, and I scavenged the ground for my morningstar. As I gave my all to find it, Lucifer's army was still fighting to its last breath.

There! My Jugulator was still fallen, only about seventy feet away from my person. As I charged toward it, I was stopped by a spear piercing my leg. I let out a cry of pain as I ripped it out and hurled it back into the crowd. It turned two demons into a kabob, and they were easily drowned out by the rest of the swarm. I turned back to my weapon to discover a lone demon trying his best to pick it up. In a fit of more fury, I yelled to him and shot toward the horrid creature at the speed of a bullet train. I could see the utter fear in his eyes as I charged, knowing that he knew his end had come. I bent my head and rolled into the scene, where as I rose, my horns impaled his sorry excuse of a body. I tore his remains off of my head, spraying even more hellfire blood on my forearm, and regained my bonebreaker of a weapon.

The mass that was Hell's army was no longer an army; it was only a group now. I continued to shatter bones and spill blood over my home. Another one of the demons' weapons slashed my left arm, and I rubbed the blood over the corpse that I turned the attacker into. Less than one hundred demons still remained, but they persisted. They were driven by the sheer power of the Devil, who was merciless against whoever went against him. He was willing to use *all* of his units to prevent any threat against his life, not that he ever needed to until now.

The group was almost unnoticeably small now; the army that was once controlled by the Devil himself was, in an instant, massacred by his own agent gone rogue. I breathed rapidly as I stood watching the rest of the weak and insufferable demons hesitantly approach me. Adrenaline was still coursing through my body. I noticed the Hellstitchers disappeared from my portal. I knew instantly they were on their way now that all of the cannon fodder had been used up. They would use the demons' damage as leverage against me, to get any edge they could gain against the Monger.

Twelve demons remained, and as they slowly started toward me, I took the opportunity to catch my breath. After a few more seconds passed, one let out a cry and flew to lacerate my face. I tilted my head just in time and immediately took a hold of her spear, using it to slam her red body into a group of stalagmites.

The other demons huddled and started to whisper amongst each other. They were devising a plan, for sure. A last-ditch effort to end my life would be the last thing they'd try to do. I suspected Lucifer had ceased his hivemind activities on the demons. If he didn't, they'd be rushing me down. But why? Why had he lost control? Had he realized his army was done for? Perhaps he was enacting a new plan, and he didn't need the demons anymore. Suprise wouldn't tame me if he was already making a plan when I arrived through the gates.

"Oh, please," I said, rolling my eyes. The crowd turned their gaze to me, wide-eyed. I was still out of breath, but I had to terminate the stragglers before they had a chance to counter.

I slowly began to stride toward them. One of the hideous demons spotted my movement and started screeching, alerting the others. They all jumped back into the air and drew their lances and tridents against me once again.

I was over it. Pissed to the bones. I'd come this far; how could these degenerates get in my way, after all that I'd been through? I sacrificed more than they could understand, and what's it all going to be worth in the end anyway?

I snatched small boulders from the ground and

maliciously chucked them at the demons. They scattered and separated themselves, running away like the cowards they really were, and that's how I knew for sure that the Devil had loosened his control on them. Perfect. That's precisely what I needed, and it was so very easy to gain.

I booked it and ran past the wimpy bodies of Hell. The rapid flapping of their wings caught my ear early, and I skidded to a stop. I swung my morningstar up to the sky, hearing a thud and the breaking of bones a split-second later. The ball fell to the dirt, as did the last aggressor. I turned my head back to see the last few demons flying away in utter fear. A fast chuckle escaped my body, and I turned back to the road in front of me. My arrogance quickly turned to dread as I saw who was waiting for me.

The last three Hellstitchers, armed to the teeth. Atrocify and his sword. Gomorrah and his cudgel. Immolatus and his chest full of scabbards, each individual scabbard holding a unique throwing knife. Classic. Almost just like old times. Though in this instance, it's a three-on-one. My odds of beating them were not high; they were not even ten percent I'd say. I let out a deep sigh as I gripped my Jugulator with an iron fist. I had to do this. If I didn't...then the doctor's death...the only thing I regretted...would be for nothing.

"The Devil is waiting, Decipere!" Atrocify shouted. "He's going to obliterate you with your own weapon! A fitting end for a heretic, I'd say."

"D-Decipere gone c-c-cuckoo crazy!" Gomorrah said, smiling without sanity. His entire body was twitching with an urge for bloodshed.

I said nothing but continued to glare at the faces of my friends. My upper lip twitched with resentment. The other two began forming a circle around me, ever so slowly. I shot a quick glance at both of them before turning back to Atrocify.

"If you came to hear me beg, you will be disappointed," I finally growled back.

"Are you sure?" he answered, a smug smile on his face.

I howled to the foes and then charged. They, too, broke out in a frenzy. The battle taking place was exasperating; I couldn't find even a half of a second to catch my breath. My morningstar continued to swing at the others, while they continued to lash out at me. I could only duck and dodge so much. A hit landed on my shoulder, a knife lobbed from Immolatus. The pain and a streak of blood scored a cry from my vocals, but I still kept up with the movements.

Finally, I landed a forceful kick into Gomorrah, knocking him into the stone wall on the other side of the fight. The opening gave me a chance to grip Immolatus' scabbards and tear them off of his body, as well as sending him into air. Suddenly, I was shoved from behind and crashed face first into the ground, with my morningstar being disarmed. I had realized quickly that Atrocify rammed me with his shield. I quickly turned around to see him lunging with his sword but rolled over with the highest speed my reflexes could give to me. His sword stuck into the ground where I once lay, and with one foul kick, I snapped the angry blade in half.

I rose back up, with only a second to gain a deep breath. Swiftly, I rushed to the broken short sword and placed the blade end into my satchel. This would give me the jump on Satan once I reached him... Suddenly, heavy pairs of footsteps came from behind me. Gomorrah was back, with Immolatus at his side. Immolatus seized Gomorrah's cudgel and swung at my head. I darted back and ducked down to avoid the strikes of madness, then let out a furious series of punches.

"Gomorrah, now!" he yelled, holding his gut as he backed off.

It wouldn't take a rocket scientist to guess what happened next. One bellowing *BOOM* from Gomorrah, and suddenly the vast battlefield became a cloud of sulfur. A cloud this size could rain over an entire human city, given the opportunity. The limited sight meant that Gomorrah was now my only enemy within this cloud, as he was the only one who knew how to do battle within it.

I gasped in fear, not being able to see any sort of terrain, weapon, or any other demon. I began to close my eyes and breathe. I knew what I had to do. Just...focus. I took a deep breath and settled myself... I waited and listened for the silent footsteps coming from my wicked companion. I held my breath and waited for any sign of movement. Any time now...

There! From my right, there was a soft crunch of dirt, so silent it couldn't have been heard by any ordinary being. I swung out a roundhouse kick to that direction, and with the force of one thousand tons, my foot connected with the psychotic cranium of Gomorrah, instantly shattering the right portion of his skull, knocking him out cold. I couldn't see, but his body dropped with a loud thud, and there were no extra sounds to suggest he was getting up. He wasn't dead, that's for sure. He had survived many worse injuries than that. I'd have to make sure to finish him off when I found my morningstar.

As the sulfur faded, the crippled body of the fifth most powerful Hellstitcher lay still. A grunt came from across the arena, from Atrocify. I then smiled and waved toward him with the upmost cocky attitude, ignoring the searing pain coming from my battle wounds. He didn't appreciate it, as he grew his shield back to full size and strode toward me.

"Come on!" I screamed as he started to run.

My smile quickly vanished, however. Out of the corner of my eye, I witnessed the bulkiest of hellfire balls I had ever laid my eyes on. With less than a second to spare, I leaped behind a large boulder I was only just fortunate enough to find. The heat of the hellfire boiled my blood to the point I was writhing in pain. I'd never felt so drained...so broken...so dead...

The heat ended, and I slowly rose to my feet. The pain didn't end there, however, as Atrocify's shield came down onto my head like a building collapsing. Stunned, I jumped to the side and fell over to the ground. Immolatus' hellfire was still searing my skin, and I didn't even think that was possible. I weakly looked up and saw my morningstar a short walk away. My morningstar!

With adrenaline kicking back up into my incandescent blood, I regained my footing and ferociously grabbed onto Immolatus, who was attempting another stab into my flesh with an extra knife he picked off the ground. I slowly raised his flailing body over my head and slammed him over my bent knee! Blood splurged from his mouth as he fell back to the ground, unable to breathe. I broke out into a sprint toward my beloved weapon and reclaimed its beauty as mine once again.

Atrocify was behind me, closing in with his invincible shield. I crashed my morningstar into it, deflecting both of our blows. He charged again, and I side-stepped and gripped his horn, tossing him away from the battle. I looked again to Immolatus to discover he was recovering from the damage I caused. He had his hands clamped over his stomach, weakly walking toward me. I yelled again, and with one last swing from my morningstar, I spun into a dynamo of destruction and blew his head clean off the shoulders.

Blood splattered my weapon, as it did the ground and my legs. Immolatus was dead. Gomorrah was next. His body lay only a few meters away from me. Breathing heavily, I trudged toward my next victim, rage fueling the tunnel vision I had focused onto him. I stopped next to his unconscious body, and I stamped his head in. Disgusting sounds of blood spewing out overwhelmed the sounds of my exhausted breathing. I continued to crush his skull into a paste, not taking the slimmest of chances of him surviving. Gomorrah's brains were staining my feet, but I didn't care. He was dead, and now I could take the next step in my plan.

I heard the sounds of Atrocify coming from behind and slowly rotated until I met eyes with him. He, too, was exhausted from the fight. Unlike him, though, I was bleeding heavily and was on the verge of fainting.

"You...were supposed...to lead us!" he cried out.

"We were partners, and you did...all of this, for what?!"

I didn't answer him. I felt lightheaded, and I couldn't understand what he was saying at this point.

"We had a good thing going, Decipere!" Atrocify breathed. "If you knew your place, and put away your pride, you wouldn't have to be executed!"

I still couldn't understand what he said to me. My vision was blurry, and my eyes were weakening. If he told me he'd let me run, I would never process it.

"I thought you as a friend, Decipere," he continued. "You helped me on my journey, all that time ago. We rose to the top together."

This, I heard. A fistful of guilt, sadness, and anger decked my mourning heart. I let out a soft groan and sunk my head. He was right. I didn't deserve to have the power I had. I certainly didn't deserve to have someone to call a friend. I never thought just how much emotion a demon could feel, but now...I felt it all.

I slowly started to approach him and weakly flailed my Jugulator around. Atrocify effortlessly caught it by the chain, only a foot in front of me. My sight was blurry... I didn't know how much longer I could stay conscious.

Atrocify yanked the weapon away from my arms, and I couldn't feel enough in my nerves to fight back. My legs shook rapidly, for the first time in my life, and perhaps the last. He walked behind me, breathing heavily with each step. Although I barely could tell what was going on, I knew what he was doing. My battle had ended, and I had to be taken to Satan. This was the plan, I reassured myself. This was the plan.

"You're done," he firmly stated to me as he threw

the chain of my morningstar over my horns and around my neck. He began to tug hard, and my hands instinctively began to claw at my throat. My life flashed before my very own eyes. I saw when I was first in battle and when I won the title of Monger. I saw the first contract I completed. I saw the doctor and his daughter. I grew sorrowful once again, and with my last conscious breath, I shed a tear.

***

I woke up, startled. I gasped for air, breathing heavily as I awoke in front of the throne. Atrocify had finally brought me to our maker. He was kneeling down, only inches away from my fallen body. I was still bleeding from every limb of my body, but I no longer felt jaded. I slowly closed my eyes and stood up. I gripped my stomach as I rose, pain still making itself known. Towering before me once again, Lucifer sat.

The Devil looked down unto me with a freezing glare of pure resentment. The molten lava was flowing from his appendages like a river current, moving faster than the speed of light. Glossy eyes paralyzed me; the fires inside them could immobilize even the mightiest of warriors. His mouth opened, revealing his clenched teeth, and he spoke.

"Insolent pup," he muttered.

I let out a yelp as he snatched me off of the ground and pulled me to his level of height. I may have been impervious to the lava flowing from his hand, but damn... He held his grip taut. I desperately tried to escape his clutches, flailing my bleeding legs around and struggling to wriggle my arms out of his fingers.

"Decipere! You have defied me for the last time!" he shrieked. "Your betrayal has led you to your death, and by your own weapon at that! Your defiance will be dealt with by the Lord of Hell, with the most fitting punishment of all!"

Lucifer opened up his opposite hand, displaying the doctor's treasured demon-slaying gun. He moved it closer to my head and shook it around, as if to taunt me. He closed the hand back up and began to shrink. I fell from the heights of plane and crashed to the floor with a loud CRACK.

Groaning, I shakily picked myself back up and lifted my head to see him at his smallest form. Still only an astounding fifteen feet tall, Lucifer gazed at the gun for what seemed like hours. He rolled it in his hands and investigated every nook and cranny. Finally, he gripped it by its vicious handle and took aim at my person. Atrocify took fear in this and took a hasty step to the side.

"What have you got to say? Any snarky remarks before I decimate you?" he asked.

I looked him in the eyes with all the hatred I could muster. I stood with my back straight and put my arms to my side. My right hand was centimeters away from the opening to my satchel, seemingly being unnoticed by Satan, due to my stance change. My teeth were seething with blood-filled rage, and I wanted nothing more than to tear the flesh off of the beast.

"Yeah, if I were t—" I suddenly cut myself off and yanked the broken sword from my satchel. Though heavily wounded, I was drowned with adrenaline and speed. Fast as lightning, I gripped the blade by the edge and leaped at Atrocify, impaling his gut with his own trophy.

The Devil yelled, caught off guard by my sudden transition from conversation to action. He clicked the trigger as quickly as he could, but nothing happened. Atrocify let out an ear-piercing howl and dropped to the rocks. He stayed lying down and didn't make a move to stand back up.

"Gah! Fire, you insolent junk of technology, fire!" Satan screamed. "Decipere, I will slay you where you stand, whether I use the gun or not!"

He began to grow again but prioritized his left hand, the one without the gun. His left hand grew faster and faster until the rest of the body was but a speck of dust in comparison. He then lifted a closed fist up, preparing to crush the heretic, and I acted swiftly.

I plunged my hand into the satchel once again, for the last time. Within it, I grabbed what I needed and ripped it out. Seconds before the weight of the closed fist collapsed onto me, I flipped the cover off of my device. The fist grew close. It was less than a second away.

All of a sudden, the switch of the doctor's failsafe had been flipped. An abrupt flash of white light erupted from the throne. And then, nothing.

Chapter Twenty

Satan's body tumbled down the cave. It fell through the walls of his throne room, disappearing into the inky black abyss below. It was all over. I peered down into the hole for a good thirty seconds before walking back to Atrocify. He was in pain, wounded from the broken blade I stuck in him. It was lodged into his gut.

I put my hand on his shoulder and gripped the hilt of his own sword. He was breathing heavily and barely standing up. He gave me a freezing-cold look before gluing his eyes to my hand. I quickly yanked it out and threw it to the rocky ground. Atrocify let out a gasp and clenched his hands on his wound. Blood found its way out of his body, oozing out through his fingers.

He tried to stand straight up but recoiled in pain. After plopping down, he finally spoke to me.

"What was this all for, Decipere?" He coughed. "Were you tired of not being the strongest force in Hell?"

"I..." I started. "I wanted to rule."

"Was *this* worth all of the effort?"

"No," I said, lowering my head.

"Was it worth all of your peers that you've killed,

that lie dead where you struck them?"

"No."

"What is it worth, then?"

"Nothing."

"Nothing?!" he lashed out. "You killed our family! They're all dead because of you! We were a force to be reckoned with for a thousand years, and we all rose to the top at the very beginning! We did that together, and you sacrificed it all for nothing?!"

"I..." I hesitated.

"You what?" Atrocify said, spitting blood. "You made a mistake? You allied yourself with an enemy instead of asking us for help? We had a good thing going, you stupid son of a bitch, but you just had to blow it up! You and your pride and ego! You just *had* to be the man!"

"Atrocify..."

"No, it doesn't matter anymore!" he yelled out before calming himself down. "Everyone's dead, and I'm losing blood. Soon, I'll be dead, too."

"I'm sorry."

"Pah!" He laughed. "You're not sorry. You never *have* been sorry for a single damn thing."

"I met a man who lived alone with his daughter. She was only eight or nine."

"And?"

"And he wanted to exterminate the Hellstitchers," I said solemnly. "I thought it was my chance to kill Satan and usurp his throne for my own. I thought it was perfect."

"What's your point in telling me this?"

"His mother was beaten and raped by her husband, and she could only use a Hellstitcher to stop him. She was being abused every day for four months straight, and her son never knew. I felt bad for the very first time. I was scared of what I felt, and I pushed it away. Within the next few hours, I killed the man I allied with. I had to. It was the contract. But...I had to murder his daughter to do it."

This caught Atrocify's attention.

"You killed a little girl just to save your sorry ass?" he asked.

"Yes," I said, eyes burning up, "I watched them die, and it utterly killed me inside. I realized just what I was."

"Decipere..." he said softly. "You realized you made a mistake, one that couldn't be forgiven."

"I never had the intention to do it. I just...ran out of time. I was scared. I was a coward!"

"So you really are sorry, aren't you?" he asked. "And you killed the rest of us just to fulfill the man's wishes, right?"

I nodded. Atrocify threw up more blood and got to his feet. He began walking away, toward the stone bridge. He wouldn't make it far at all.

"You finally got what you deserved, Decipere," he said as he stumbled away. "Hopefully your humility will show you into a better life. You have the rest of time and the entirety of Hell at your disposal. I am glad to die for this."

"Atrocify..." I called.

He looked back, awaiting my final message.

"Thank you...for, um..." I struggled. "For being yourself. Even when I was busy in my self-absorption, you were still helping me. I had no right to receive it."

He rolled his eyes and walked away. My stomach

ached the more blood that dropped from him.

"Goodbye, Decipere," he said.

I closed my eyes and furrowed my brow in anger and disappointment. I didn't want to lose Atrocify; he was the last I had. I never realized just how valuable he was to me, until he had to go. I supposed I did deserve it, even if he didn't.

He walked away for another minute. Every step he took I thought would be his last, but he's the strongest among us. If anyone could keep going, it would be him. My fight was over, and I was done. Done with everything. He was still going, and he walked with confidence. My heart sank as he froze up and fell over. The flames ignited from his horns went out completely, replaced by utter despair. No movement ever came from him.

My heart was empty. I felt numb as I looked around the empty cave. Nothing here remained, and nothing could be done. Hell was dead, and I killed it. There was nothing to do and no one to interact with. There was nothing to live for. The only two options I had now were to either die or sit here for an eternity.

There was one thing I could do before I make my decision, however. Splitting a bloodportal open, I finally gathered the courage to move from my spot. I took a step inside and disappeared.

Epilogue: Epitaph

I stepped out on a familiar lawn, furrowing my brow as I arrived. The sun was rising, and the sky above glowed in reds and yellows. It was purely divine.

I stepped through the tall grass to see the gigantic hole I made in the side of their house was not yet repaired. It was boarded up, with light wooden planks comfortably covering it all over. I was at the house of Rodney Whitewinter.

I took small steps to his house, almost regretting showing up here in the first place. I didn't want to face him, not again. He was by far the worst contract I'd had to endure for years. That being said, I couldn't blame him for the events that took place here. He was only a stupid teenager, trying to impress the bully. In a way, it reminded me of Tenebris. Both of them deserved vengeance unto my person, and they would have it eventually.

Phasing myself inside, I spotted a woman preparing some kind of meal within the kitchen. She was wearing a red apron and had her long brunette hair up in a bun. That must be Whitewinter's mother. Should I ask her about Rodney's whereabouts, she would cry in terror at the sight of a demon. I didn't have any Sulfric Growler capsules anyway. I had to move up to Rodney's room.

A second away from moving to the stairs, I saw a boy walk out from a different room and join his mother in the kitchen. It was Rodney. He began cutting vegetables and preparing them in small bowls. I noticed his hands were shaking as if he was nervous about something. It couldn't be easy trying to live an anxiety-free life after going through what he did. I utterly traumatized both him and his friend, only to feel a slight ounce of joy in myself. I felt sorry for him.

I came up the stairway and searched around for Rodney's bedroom. The first door I opened yielded the room I was looking for, allowing me to sit inside and await Rodney's arrival. I had to apologize to him in some way, but I knew I could never be forgiven by him, even if the child I killed was a bully. He deserved what came to him, and I stood by it, but it never gave me the right to do such a thing.

For minutes and minutes I waited, until the bedroom door finally opened. Rodney made his way inside and locked the door behind him. He looked to the floor and began walking to his bed before glancing in my direction, finally catching me in his room. He froze, eyes widening. I considered speaking to him, but I wanted him to have the first move.

"H-Hellstitcher," he whispered. "W-Why are you back?"

"Rodney, I, erm..." I started, struggling to spit out what I wanted to say. "In the last few hours, I've made multiple mistakes, and it made me realize how horrendously awful I treated the ones around me, you included."

"Yeah, you tore my friend in half," he said, rightfully angry. "Right in front of me. You blew out my tire and made my car roll into a ditch. I can't even afford to pay for the damage. Finding a job is difficult, and even when I find one, I won't have a car to get there."

"I'm sorry, Rodney," I said, matching his passion. "Were I the demon I was a few days ago, I would have told you to deal with it. But alas, I am not."

"Then what are you here for?" he asked. "Just to tell me you're sorry? Do you realize how much that *doesn't* help?"

"No, I have something for you," I said, opening my satchel. "This is your friend's gold Rolex watch. I kept it safe, but I feel it would be better for you to have it."

Rodney slowly approached, eyeing the precious watch within my massive hand. He seemed to stare at it for a thousand ages, just admiring the sheer beauty of it.

"You...want to give me Brad's watch that you stole?" he asked.

"I'm returning it to you," I said apologetically. "I don't know how else to make it up to you."

"You could buy me a new car, if you wanted."

"No, I couldn't, even if I wanted," I told him. "I don't have human money. I only have this to give to you. At most, you can sell it or place it on Brad's tombstone, or... It's your watch now. You decide what to do with it."

"Uh, thanks, Hellstitcher," he said quietly. "I guess."

"Yeah," I said in an awkward tone. "I wish I could have done more, but I don't know just what I can do."

"Well, do you know anything about carpentry?" he asked, raising his head up. "My wall still needs to be fixed."

"No, but if you give me a list of everything you need, I could steal it," I said jokingly.

"Right." He chuckled. "There's not really anything you can do for me, Hellstitcher. But the thought really makes me feel better about that night. I'm going to sell the watch and hopefully make enough money to pay for my car. If it's not enough, don't worry about it."

"I understand. I won't be around for long, so I need you to assure me there's nothing else I can do."

"Yeah, it's all right," he said. "Thank you."

I bowed to him and turned around, facing the boarded-up wall. I crouched down and leaped at it at full speed, phasing through the wood with ease. I landed back into the tall grass and took another look at the house, remembering the bloody night that only happened less than a week ago.

I continued on my way, striding through the lawn until I met my bloodportal again. Feeling its cold embrace, I pushed myself through and wound up on another familiar driveway. Though this time, it was where my biggest mistake took place. The air was lukewarm, and I could barely feel it on my rocky skin. This place was my legacy now.

I walked to the middle of the lawn, where the doctor and his daughter still lay. I let out a sigh of shame and gently picked up the doctor's body. I set him down by the porch stairs, closing his eyes manually in the process. I proceeded to lift his daughter off of the stakes, spilling blood as I slowly detached her from the wood. I set her down next to her father and closed her eyes as well.

With little left to do, I began grabbing at the

earth below and dug a hole. I kept digging until it was slightly above the size of a human, making sure it was deep enough to fit the two of them. After less than an hour, I was done with the hole.

I set multiple flat rocks inside, enough to cover the entire dirt layer. I lifted the doctor first and elegantly placed him inside, with his hands to his sides. Lila was next; I set her on top of her father and entwined their hands together. He was now holding her close, and she held him back with love. The hands covered the hole in her stomach; I could not bear to see the destruction I caused anymore.

I came back to the house and tore off wooden planks from the porch. After gathering enough, I placed them at the side of the tomb and wedged them together to completely enclose it. I started shoveling the dug-up dirt and began burying it back into the earth. After it was completely covered, I made sure to leave a slight mound in the dirt to let others know the dead rested here. Once the police found them, they would be placed into better graves. For now, mine would keep them safe.

I wasn't done yet. I had gathered two large stones and began carving into it with another rock. One stone bore the doctor's name, and the other presented Lila's. I dug them into the head of the mound and continued my work.

I gathered multiple twigs, enough to fill my arms and my satchel, and set them all down beside me. Slowly picking them up one by one, I continued spelling out the phrase that hit me harder than truck. After it was done, I sat down in front of it and spoke to the dead.

"You never deserved this. You and your daughter never deserved the blood I spilled from you. I thought I could take what I wanted and treat anyone how I wanted to treat them. I took advantage of you, and I ended up with nothing. Nothing but an empty cave and dead family. That's what *I* deserve. You may rest well knowing your quest will be finished. The other Hellstitchers are dead. I took it even further, too. I killed the Librarian, Cerberus, and Satan as well. They're all dead. When I killed the Librarian, I admit it wasn't for this purpose: it was a move to get Satan angry. But...if I hadn't killed her before, I would have ended her after it was all over. I am overwhelmed with guilt, and I needed to atone for what I've done. I am aware atonement and redemption is never possible, but again, I deserve this. The only thing to do now is finish what you and your mother started. The only Hellstitcher left is me, and I need to let myself go. I just don't know when I'll have the courage to do it. When I die, I have no idea where I'll end up. I could cease to exist, for all I know. It's for the best. Rest well, Lila. And rest well, Silvestre Kallus."

I finished my work and rested my eyes upon it. The morning sun's rays shined down on the tombstones, illuminating their names further. I felt a slight breeze wave over my body and melt my heart away. The trees echoed the cries of souls lost today, and the house lay barren of life.

I took a step back and took one last look at the hearty grave. It was tragic and saddening, but ultimately, it was the harsh reality. Returning to my bloodportal, I read the heap of twigs one last time.

"Hold on to my heart."

HELLSTITCHER by Silver Skye

THANK YOU

You can reach the author by email at
smelkerkyle@gmail.com

Please leave a review on Amazon or the contact page at
WickedHarvestBooks.com

Share with family and friends.

Please visit

WickedHarvestBooks.com
LastLeafPublishing.com
EditsByJessica.com

HELLSTITCHER by Silver Skye

Made in the USA
Monee, IL
24 April 2025

16321834R00134